THE GUNSMITH

#57

CROSSFIRE MOUNTAIN

The Gunsmith by J.R. Roberts

THE GUNSMITH

#57

CROSSFIRE MOUNTAIN

J.R. ROBERTS

SPEAKING VOLUMES, LLC
NAPLES, FLORIDA
2014

THE GUNSMITH
#57 CROSSFIRE MOUNTAIN

Copyright © 1986 by Robert J. Randisi

ISBN 978-1-61232-660-3

Chapter One

The Gunsmith rode into Tucson, Arizona looking for nothing more than a cool beer and maybe a little female companionship. It was June and already hot, with the daytime temperatures nudging one hundred degrees. Clint had been here before, and he knew that he wanted to be somewhere else by the time July rolled around.

He was a handsome man in his thirties with just enough age on his rugged face to get him a second look. Some men get better looking with a few wrinkles and Clint was lucky enough to be one. He had a prominent jaw and a nice, even smile that could be disarming. Unless you knew him pretty well, he seemed so casual and easy going that it was hard to believe that he was the famous Gunsmith. Clint preferred anonymity, but he was too well known across the West to get it very often. A lot of men had challenged him for his unwanted fame, and almost as many had died for their foolishness. Clint considered himself a peaceful man until riled, a man who would go a good distance out of his way to avoid trouble—though most strangers would not have believed that.

He just didn't look like your ordinary run-of-the-mill gunslinger. He dressed nicely, good clothes, a fine pair of custom-made boots by a renowned bootmaker in El Paso, and a black Stetson hat that was new enough not

1

to be marred by a sweatstain around the hat-band. He was clean shaven, too. Whenever possible, Clint made it a point to get a barbershop shave every day and a hair-cut at least once a month.

But Clint Adams was not a peacock or even a dandy. He eschewed gaudy clothes and fancy hatbands like some men wore to attract attention. On his hip he wore a well-oiled Colt .45 in a no-nonsense holster that was dry as a buffalo bone and created no friction whatso-ever when he was unloading his sixshooter.

Unlike a lot of traveling men, when Clint rode into a town, he did not head directly for the nearest watering hole, or prostitute, or even hotel. Instead, Clint always made it a point to search out the best livery for his horse, Duke. The black gelding was as much a friend as a means of transportation. He and that horse had ridden a lot of lean and dangerous trails together. Sometimes, even a fast man with a gun has to save his own skin by escaping rather than fighting. Duke had both speed and endurance.

The first livery looked run down and poor so Clint kept going. The second looked to be in good repair, but when Clint poked around back he saw that the corrals were hock-deep in manure, and some of the horses were underfed. He was getting worried when at last he found a stable that finally met his high standards. The place was whitewashed, the corrals clean and the horses all looked well fed. Clint rode up to a pile of hay and dis-mounted. He picked a stem of the alfalfa and poked it into his mouth then chewed it thoughtfully. It was good and fresh, no mold, and with enough leaf in it to meet Duke's pleasure.

"Howdy," the liveryman said. "You like to eat hay, mister?"

The man was in his late fifties and smiling at his own joke. There was no malice in his eyes and Clint chuckled. "I'll tell you," he confessed. "There have been times when I wished I could eat hay. Lean times."

"I know what you mean. Mighty fine animal you got there."

"Thanks. I wouldn't trust him to just anyone to keep."

The liveryman grew serious. "There's not a better stable than mine in all of Arizona," he said with a firm voice. "I feed the best and I feed plenty. Grain is two bits a day extra."

"Grain him," Clint said handing his reins to the man and following him inside where it was cool and dark. A cat meowed and brushed up against his leg and you could hear the lazy drone of flies as they darted in and out of the shafts of sunlight poking through the walls. The interior of the barn conformed to Clint's initial good impression. All the tack and tools were hung on nails and hooks, the hayloft was solid, and every saddle was covered with a burlap sack to keep it from the dust.

"You be stayin' long, mister?" the liveryman asked, noting Clint's look of approval.

"Couple days at the most. Gets a little too hot in this country for me."

"Me too," the liveryman confessed, "but a man has to make a livin' year around, don't he?"

"Yeah, I guess he does at that."

"What be your trade?"

"I'm a gunsmith."

"You don't look like no gunsmith to me but I sure wouldn't call you a liar."

The assessment was bold but true enough. Clint had left his gunsmithing wagon in Texas when he had gotten tired of driving a team of horses and decided that it was time he sat astride a horse rather than the hard, bumpy seat of a wagon. Besides, the gunsmithing was something he did more for enjoyment than to make a living. After

4

being a lawman for many years, he had salted away a
few dollars and there were enough men and women in
the West that owed him half their lives so that he never
had to worry if times got hard again.

"Where's the best hotel and saloon?"

"You lookin' for. . . ."

"Peace and quiet," Clint said. "And I guess if there
was a pretty face around, that wouldn't be too bad
either."

The liveryman grinned. "You sorta look like a ladies
man. You a gambler?"

"A gunsmith, remember?"

"Oh sure," the man said not believing a word of it.
"Well, best hotel in town is the Antelope just up the
street. Costs two dollars a night but I hear it's worth it.
Change the sheets for every new customer."

Clint had a smile. "Sounds like my kind of hotel.
What about a saloon?"

"The Blue Dog is what you are probably lookin' for.
Beer costs more than rare pigeon piss, fifty cents a glass,
but they keep it in the cellar so it is the coolest in town.
Whiskey is good, not that crap the Apache make and
sell to the cheap joints and is half mescale, half taran-
tula poison. If it don't kill ya, it'll drive you insane."

"Blue Dog sounds fine," Clint said thinking how
good a cool beer would taste. "Much obliged for the information and here's a little extra for brushing the sweat
and dirt off of my horse."

"Well thank you!" the liveryman said, tucking the
dollar into his bib overalls. "Ain't you going to ask me
where the whorehouses are in this town?"

"Nope. I never pay for what a woman is willing to
give me for free."

The liveryman chuckled. "Goddamn but you're a
cocky sonofabitch all right! Ain't no free women in this
town, not that I know of. But if there were, I'd guess

5

you'd be the man to smell 'em out, right?''

Clint was no braggart but he did wink. "We'll see."

"Goddamn! What I wouldn't do to be young again like you and not always smelling like horseshit and mules! Goddamn!''

Clint headed for the door with his rifle in one hand and his saddlebags strung across his left shoulder. He stepped out in the bright sunshine and felt the temperature rise ten degrees as the sun blasted off the hard-packed dirt street. "You keep my horse in the shade," he called back into the gloom.

"Yes sir, mister gunsmith! I'll put him right here in this stall and if you pay me another dollar, I'll even swish the flies away from him so he don't even have to lift his own tail!''

An hour later he climbed out of a cool bath and felt like a new man. The water was black now, evidence of the long trail he had ridden. Clint pulled on his pants and buckled his gunbelt. He grabbed his boots and combed his dark hair with his long, supple fingers. Then, he opened the door and padded down the hallway and back to his room. He had left a match propped up against the door beside the frame and it was still standing so he knew that he had not had any unannounced visitors.

Someday I'll act like a normal person instead of being so suspicious, he told himself knowing that he would never change. For too many long years he had hunted and been hunted. A man either developed a sixth sense and suspicious ways, or he wound up a resident of Boot Hill. And once suspicious, always suspicious. Sure, there were a lot of men who owed him their lives, but there were just as many who had sworn to kill him given the chance to do so safely from his backside or in ambush.

Clint went inside and unpacked his clean shirt and

6

underclothes. He dressed again, pressing his pants with a wet towel until they looked fresh. Then he buckled on his gunbelt once more. He studied himself in the mirror and when he decided that he would not scare anyone or anything with his looks, he headed for the Blue Dog Saloon wondering just what entertainment the night would bring.

Chapter Two

The Blue Dog Saloon was exactly right for Clint. It had a touch of class, but was not ostentatious. The interior was adorned with pictures of horses, men—and a huge blue dog. It was a short-haired and ugly thing with fangs that the artist had obviously exaggerated. The painting hung in an immense gold leaf frame right in the center of the back-bar under the cash register. Quite obviously, it was considered to be the saloon's prize picture.

"Never seen a dog that color," Clint remarked when he sidled up to the bartender.

The man grinned and wiped his sweaty brow with a thick forearm. "Not many have, stranger. That there is a Queensland Blue Heeler, a cattle dog of which there is no equal in America. Best dog I ever saw or owned. Saved my life once."

Clint asked the obligatory question. "How?"

"I was making love to a married woman and damned if her gunfighter husband didn't ride back that night two whole days early. That fine dog of mine warned me and even then I was too slow to get up in time. I would have had my butt shot off except for the blue dog saved my life. He jumped straight for the man's throat. Took the bullet meant for me and fell dying on the floor. Even so, he managed to grab the gunfighter's boot top and pull him off balance so that he kept missing me."

"And what did you do?"

"I was on my way out the window, of course! Next day I found my blue dog and he'd been castrated and hung upside down on a picket fence. I took that as a message and lit out of town, but not before I took the blue dog and buried him deep and proper."

"Touching story," Clint said cryptically. "Now how about a cool beer."

"Cost you fifty cents."

"Fine, I'll take it anyway."

"Figured you might. You lookin' for a little action, stranger? Cards? Women, maybe a little of both, huh?"

"A beer will do for starters." He had never seen a town with so many nosy people asking what he was looking for.

The bartender and saloon owner acted disappointed but nodded. "Anyway," he said, reaching under the bar for a bottle of beer that was resting in a tub of cool water, "you asked about the painting and I told you. I owe that Queensland Blue Heeler my life and I learned a good lesson—don't ever get caught screwing a gunfighter's wife!"

"No chance," Clint said, wishing the man would stop talking so much and get the damned beer. "I stay clear away from married women. There's just too many good looking single ones."

"That's for sure," the saloonkeeper said, placing Clint's beer on the bar. "Fifty cents, please."

Clint paid and drank the beer faster than he had planned. It was cool and as good as he had tasted in a long while. "I'll have another," he said.

"Comin' right up!"

He took his time with the second beer. At fifty cents a bottle, you did not swill the stuff like water. Clint eased around and rested his elbows on the bar and studied the beginning of the evening crowd. There were about thirty men in the Blue Dog and most of them looked to be the merchants and more respectable citizens of Tucson. The place had a nice, comfortable feel to it; no one looked like the kind to get drunk or belligerent so Clint relaxed. There were three or four women serving drinks to the poker stables and Clint sized them up with a practiced eye. He was not excited about any of them in particular, but neither would he have said no to any of them.

"Say there!" a man shouted from across the room.

"Aren't you . . . yes, by damned! You're the Gunsmith!"

All eyes turned and the conversation died. Clint cussed silently, for now several more men in the room recognized him and the place was suddenly astir. It was a shame, Clint thought, that a man could not even enjoy a couple beers in peace anymore.

The loud mouth hurried over with a couple of other men in tow. He was about sixty, with a wild bush of silver muttonchop whiskers and a fine silver-tipped mustache. "My name is P.T. Baker," he announced. "And I just happen to own the finest hotel in this great city. The Baker Hotel would welcome your business."

Clint shifted uncomfortably. "Sorry, I'm already lodged at the Antelope Hotel."

The man cringed as if he'd discovered a maggot in his meal. "My God, Gunsmith, that dump? Remove yourself from there at once and come over to an abode of class and distinction."

"Can't. Already paid."

"Then tomorrow night."

"Maybe." Clint noted that Baker sure hadn't said anything about a free room for a distinguished guest. But he did not wish to insult Baker by pointing out this fact so he sipped his beer and said nothing hoping that the man would return to his table.

"Well, I hope we have the honor of your occupancy, Mr. Gunsmith. May I buy you a drink?"

"All right. Another beer will be fine."

Baker ordered far too loudly. "One here for my good friend and the fastest gun in the West!"

He started to put his arm across the Gunsmith's shoulder, saw the look in Clint's eye and changed his mind and began talking very rapidly. "My friends, I saw the Gunsmith kill three men in a stand-up gunfight in Reno, Nevada five years ago. And I said then, P.T., that is the fastest man alive. Yep! I said that and I have never seen the equal to this man since. Show them your speed of hand, Gunsmith."

"What?"

The expansive smile slipped on P.T. Baker's meaty face. "I said, show my friends how fast you are, sir."

"Go to hell, P.T."

"What! Sir, that is no. . . ."

Clint had taken about enough of this overbearing hotel owner and so he placed his beer on the bar and then grabbed P.T. firmly by the collar and propelled him back toward the table. Immediately, the entire saloon broke into applause and laughter telling Clint that everyone found P.T. Baker a loudmouth and braggart.

"Well, goddammit!" the man raged, when he recovered his balance, "that was a hell of a nasty way to treat a man who bought you a fifty cent beer!"

Clint dug into his pants and pulled out fifty cents and pitched it to the man's feet. "Now we're even," he said, his voice edged with steel. "I don't like strangers figuring they own me for a beer or for any other damn thing. Now shut up, sit down, and leave me alone so I can enjoy myself."

Clint turned his back on the room, but he could watch every move in the bar mirror. He saw men and women staring at him and he guessed he had let the heat and too many long hours in the saddle rub his patience a little thin. Normally, he would have politely told a man like Baker to shut up and mind his own business.

Clint raised his beer and drained it as he stared at the big blue dog painting. Stupid lookin' thing, he thought. Furthermore, he did not believe that any foreign dog could hold a candle to an American one—especially when its color was so damned odd.

He drained his beer and headed for the door aware that everyone watched him. Within an hour, the word would be out all over town that the Gunsmith was staying at the Antelope Hotel. Any young fool who was ready to risk dying for a gunslinger's reputation would come searching for him either tonight or first thing in the morning.

Clint headed for the nearest cafe. He could use a good steak and some mashed potatoes with gravy. Wash it down with another beer and then maybe finish the evening off with a slice of apple pie for dessert. He knew better than to go prowling tonight for a woman because anyone seeking trouble would find him first.

Maybe he'd just buy a newspaper and a good cigar and call it an early evening. He would ride out at daybreak and then decide where he wanted to go next.

Chapter Three

Clint found a seat in the busiest cafe in town, going on the assumption that people do not flock to cafes where the food is poor. He had no sooner sat down than two boys about twelve and ten years of age came bursting in the door and raced up to his table.

"Mr. Gunsmith, will you show us your sixgun and give us your autograph!" the older one of the pair blurted, trying to catch his breath.

They were a pair of ragamuffins, poorly dressed and shoeless as he had once been. "Sure," he said, "got anything to write with?"

They didn't, not paper or pencil. They looked crestfallen until a very attractive waitress came over and said, "Josh, you and Petey go on and pester someone else! Leave this poor man to eat in peace!"

"But he's the Gunsmith!" Josh cried. "He's the most famous man that ever came to Tucson! Please, Miss Milly, he said he wouldn't care!"

They looked so desperate that the young waitress softened. She gazed down at Clint. "I'm sorry," she apologized. "I don't like anyone being bothered when they are in my place."

"No bother," Clint said with a smile, liking what he saw. Miss Milly was in her mid-twenties with straw-colored hair and topaz-blue eyes. She had a scattering of freckles across her upturned nose and she was cute, but not in a girlish way. Not when your eyes dropped a few inches and you noticed how she filled out her white blouse. About five and a half feet tall, she was well endowed and small waisted.

"Are you sure?"

"Yes. But we need something to write with."

She gave him a pen and when they touched, Clint felt that infallible tingle pass between them that never lied which said she was interested—if he was interested. Her fingers lingered for a moment touching his and then she fluttered her lashes. "So, you are the Gunsmith, huh?"

"In the flesh."

"Even I have heard of you. It's an honor to make your acquaintance and have you eat here."

"Come on, Miss Milly! We asked him first!"

Milly gave him some paper and Clint signed his name for the two boys. Then, he showed them his sixgun and their eyes bugged. "Wow! How many men has this killed?"

The Gunsmith's smile died on his lips. "Too many. I wish I had never had to use it on a single man, but when I did, I always made sure they either deserved it, or I had no choice but to defend myself."

"Will you stand up and show us your draw?" Josh asked hopefully.

Clint shook his head. By now, the entire room had forgotten their meals and conversations. Everyone was watching him. "Sorry, boys. The kind of man I admire—and you should too—never shows off."

"Yeah, but. . . ."

"Let's put it this way," Clint said patiently. "If you were a gambler in a high-stakes poker game and someone dealt you a royal flush, would you tell all the other players at your table?"

"No, but. . . ."

"Well, a gunfighter is just the same way. A real one is never stupid enough to show his hand, not until all the bets are down on the table and it's time to show your cards."

Petey, though only ten, understood poker. "Wow," he whispered. "A royal flush! You must be the fastest man with a gun alive."

"There is always someone coming up who is a hair faster. I just haven't met him yet and now all I want is just to enjoy a good steak and maybe a little wine instead of beer. Can you do that, Miss Milly?"

Her hand brushed his shoulder and, somehow, it felt very intimate to Clint.

"Just watch me. I'll cook you up the biggest, juiciest steak in the place. Corn bread, black-eyed peas and mashed potatoes with gravy. Going to make your mouth water. I hope you're very hungry, Gunsmith."

"Clint," he said. "Just Clint."

"However you like," she said with a wink that made his toes wriggle with anticipation. She turned to the boys. "Now go on and skedaddle on out of here, the both of you!"

They raced outside and after a few minutes, the room returned to normal. Clint was famished. He glanced at the other tables and the steaks looked and smelled wonderful. They were big too, and from the pulled up notch on his belt he knew that he was down about five pounds from his normal weight. The desert did that to a man, pinched him up in the belly and left him panting and washed out.

"Here's your wine and some sourdough bread to munch on while you wait for the steak," Milly told him sweetly, setting a beer glass full of burgundy on the table. "Now you just relax and I'll be along as soon as I can with your dinner."

"Take your time," he answered, wishing he could stand up and take a peek down the front of her blouse without being too obvious.

For the next half hour, he sat quietly and sipped the wine and mostly, just enjoyed the feeling of being clean and left to his own thoughts. It was good for a man to have an excellent meal served by a pretty young woman. Even if you never did a thing with her but smile at each other, it was worth plenty. It gave him a nice feeling inside that said he was still young enough to feel the sap of youth.

The time he waited seemed like no more than the snap of his fingers and then he was digging into one of the finest steaks he'd ever had.

"How is it?" Milly asked anxiously.

"Delicious!"

She beamed. "Wait until you taste my pumpkin pie."

Clint had sort of been looking forward to apple pie but you'd never have known it by his reaction. "Well, if you made it, then it has to be the best I'm ever going to taste, Milly."

She blushed. "God, but you're a sweet-tongued devil." She sashayed off, hips swinging, a big grin on her generous mouth.

Three hours later, she shut the cafe down even though it was only nine o'clock and some of the last customers complained about being rushed through their dinners, then shoved out the door.

Clint hadn't moved. He was working on his fourth glass of wine and feeling just fine. And when Milly rushed out the last griping customer and then locked the door and pulled the shutters, he was feeling even happier.

She had worked hard and her yellow hair was plastered wetly to her forehead. The kitchen was warm and when the cook left a few minutes later with a knowing grin, Milly poured herself a glass of wine joining Clint at his table.

"I've never known a gunfighter with your kind of reputation before, Clint. Most of the ones I've seen wore peach fuzz on their cheeks and swaggered around bragging about how fast they were. You don't brag at all, do you?"

"Nope. Men good at what they do never brag. They let their actions speak for themselves and that makes a whole lot more sense." Clint touched her glass to his own and said, "I get tired of people asking me questions. Mind if I ask you one or two?"

She laughed softly. "Why not? I've nothing to hide. But I'm afraid that, to a man like yourself, it would be very boring."

"I'm never bored by a pretty woman," he told her in a way that made her sit up a little straighter.

"And you think I'm pretty?"

"Of course you are. And you know it, don't you." It was not a question. Milly was a sensuous hunk of woman and one any man would like to love.

She blushed and nodded. "I do get a look and a pinch now and then," she conceded. "And there's been a man or two who thought they had me roped, but they were wrong."

"Why haven't you gotten married?"

"Oh, I will one of these days. But I like being single just fine. Besides, my father left me this business when he died and I do very well for myself. If I marry then I'll have to split the profits with a husband who probably will never come near the place and expect me to do all the work."

It made sense. A woman had damn few property rights in the West. When she married, what she owned almost always became her husband's. "You ever marry, Clint?"

"Nope."

"Come close a few times I'll bet."

He grinned. "How did you guess?"

"I just could. A man as famous and handsome as yourself is bound to have women falling all over themselves to go to bed and snare you."

"Gunfighters don't make very good husbands, Milly."

"Might not last long," she reasoned out loud, "but at least it would be exciting. Right Clint?"

She leaned forward across the table so that her lips were just inches from his own. Clint looked deep into her eyes. "Right."

They kissed hungrily. Her kiss was wet and her tongue insistent. Clint was half pulled out of his chair. Their glasses of wine crashed and spilled across the checkered tablecloth. He felt the wine dribble down onto his pants and soak through to the skin.

"Maybe we ought to get out of here and go to my hotel room," he said, pulling free. "Sure be more comfortable."

She was already breathing hard. "Can't. I got a reputation to uphold in Tucson. Got to be on the sly about this."

That didn't wash with Clint. Anyone with a pair of eyes and the brain of a small child could have seen and figured out why Milly had closed early.

"Well, where can we go then?" he asked.

"Nowhere that eyes wouldn't follow us," she breathed. "I want you right here in my place."

"You mean . . ."

"I mean on this table, under this table, all over, Clint darling."

He was amazed, but then, he had never had a woman on a cafe table and maybe it was good to do things different now and then. Clint yanked the soaked tablecloth away and dishes and silverware clattered to the floor and broke into small pieces. But Milly didn't care. She blew all the lamps out but one which she turned down very low. Then, she pulled off her dress and let it fall right in the pile of shattered dinnerware.

Clint felt a little silly undressing in a dining room, but a man had to seize opportunity wherever and however it came his way.

Chapter Four

Millie pulled two tables together so that there was enough room for her to lie part ways down. But she was in such a hurry for him that she left her legs dangling so Clint moved right up and into her, prodding and teasing her womanhood until she began to moan and move around on the table.

"Come on," she begged, lifting her head and pleading with him, "put it in all the way, now!"

He butted his hips forward. The big head of his cock slipped inside her and he rotated his hips around and around, watching her smile grow wider and wider. Her breasts were big and the nipples standing up hard. Clint poked deeper and she gasped with pleasure. Then he leaned over and began to suck on her nipples while his hips kept up the rhythm.

Her legs began to wave and she tried to lift them high enough to lock them around his hips and draw him in all the way but she could not. Her head was rocking back and forth and her eyes were wide open and slightly glazed.

"What are you trying to do to me, Clint? You're driving me crazy," she whispered breathlessly.

He laughed softly and sucked a little harder while his hips began to piston with increasing force. They moved in a tight ellipsis. She was hot and wet and Milly

19

suddenly began to stiffen. She made a funny sound deep in her throat and then she tore his mouth from her breast and kissed him deeply. She cried like an animal and began to buck wildly and Clint knew that she was almost touching her moment of ecstacy. He started driving deeper and harder into her and he could feel her body responding with its own wild violence.

"Harder," she moaned. "Clint, deeper!"

He buried himself into her and lost himself completely in the act. They began to pound at each other, hips jerking and ramming, breath coming faster and faster, hearts beating wildly.

"Ohhhh, yes!" she screamed as her body began to spasm uncontrollably and he sent his hot seed into her steamy depths. "Yes!"

He came in big, lusting spurts and she kept milking him until, at last, they lay draped across the table, spent and sweaty. She had one arm wrapped tightly around his neck but the fingernails of her other hand were biting into his buttocks.

At the height of their climax, Clint hadn't even felt her sharp fingernails but he sure did now. He reached back and grabbed her hand, certain each of her nails was drawing blood. But she had been good, very good and from the way she was already starting to squirm and nibble at his ear, Clint had a hunch she expected another repeat performance very, very soon.

"Oh but this table top is hard," she whispered. "I'll take a bed any day."

He eased off of her, lost his balance and rolled off the table to strike the floor. If that wasn't bad enough, she began to giggle hysterically. Pulling together his wounded pride, Clint climbed to his feet. Then he started to laugh.

"No more table tops, Milly."

"Agreed!"

She reached down and grabbed his cock and began

using it to tickle the soft wetness between her legs. He was surprised to see himself growing very stiff again very soon.

She tongued away a bead of sweat from her upper lip. "Are you ready again?"

He nodded, wanting her even more now than before. The second helping was always slower, and better. Clint wasn't ready for the floor though. He grabbed her and turned her around then marched over to another table and she knew without being told what he wanted her to do. She bent over at the waist and spread her legs wide. She had a fine looking butt. He stepped in close and slid his cock up and under and back into her juiciness. His right hand moved around in front and found her nub of pleasure and began to stroke it gently.

"Uhhh," she moaned and shook.

Clint shut his eyes and let his hips work against her buttocks. It was heavenly. Around and around, the feeling for them both growing stronger and stronger. The heat becoming a fire that they were both stoking.

And then suddenly, she was grabbing his hand and cock and working them deeper and harder and then she threw her head back and cried out, "Oh . . . oh, yes, Clint now!"

He obeyed, holding back nothing and driving her and the table forward across the room as they climaxed together. She moaned and collapsed forward on the table, gasping for breath, her hips quivering.

Clint staggered back feeling a little weak in the knees. He started to say something and that's when the cafe door shook with someone hammering it violently.

"Milly!" the voice shouted. "I hear you in there. What is going on! You with someone, Milly? Answer me or so help me God I'll come in shooting!"

Clint stared at the door, then at Milly. He leapt for his pants and hissed, "Who the hell is that man!"

"It's . . . it's my fiance," she sobbed, trying to pull

her panties on but tripping and falling. "He's crazy jealous!"

"Well why did you . . . oh, shit, never mind," Clint stormed. "I got to get out of here!"

The pounding grew louder. "Is it the Gunsmith, Milly! Is it him that's diddling you behind my back! I'll kill him! I'll get my men and we'll riddle that sneaky sonofabitch."

Clint heard the sound of retreating bootsteps. He was buttoning his pants, grabbing his gunbelt and searching for his boots in the dimly lit cafe.

"What did he mean, 'his men'!"

Milly began to cry. "I'm sorry. I didn't think he'd find out about us. And I thought that, if he did, he wouldn't dare come after a man like you."

"Who is he?"

She covered her face with her hands. "He's the sheriff of Tucson," she sobbed. "And he has four deputies!"

"Oh, Jesus Christ!" Clint swore, slamming his foot into one boot without bothering to find his socks. "This is all I need—five lawmen coming after me with guns! Why weren't you honest enough to tell me you were engaged! And to the sheriff, of all people!"

She pulled her dress on and sniveled. "I couldn't help it, Clint. I was never screwed by anyone famous before. And when I saw how handsome you were and the way you looked at me, I just went to jelly inside."

Clint heard the sound of running boots coming down the boardwalk. "There better be a back door to this place or I'm a goner."

"There is!" she cried. "Oh, Clint, I'm so sorry. I never knew he was that jealous. But that just proves that he really must love me, huh? Maybe I ought to get married."

As they hurried through the dining room and then the kitchen toward the back door, Clint thought about how horny and eager she had been and how being engaged had been the farthest thing from mind. "I don't think you're the marrying kind, Milly. Not yet anyway. If you marry that sheriff, some poor sucker like me is going to get killed for sure some day."

"Here it is," she said, throwing the bolt and pulling the door open. She grabbed him as he started through and gave him a passionate kiss. "It was worth it even if he shoots me instead of you," she said, wriggling those lovely breasts against his chest.

Clint pried her arms loose. Considering the seriousness of their circumstances, he guessed he should have been flattered. But he was not. Milly had gotten him into a tight fix and the last thing he wanted to do was to get involved in a shootout with the law over a lawman's woman.

"Goodbye," he said, pulling away and then looking in both directions down the alley. "It was damn good, Milly. But if I were you, I'd either get another fiance, or stay true to the one I had. Try and stall them!"

He hurried out into the darkness just as he heard the front door of the cafe being attacked. Glass shattered and Clint was racing down the dark alley. They would be after him in less than three minutes no matter what Milly did or said. And they'd know that he was staying at the Antelope Hotel.

If I had any brains at all, I'd go right to my horse and get out of here leaving my rifle and things in the hotel room and counting myself lucky to be alive. But I've got no brains and besides, I'm not the one who was at fault, Milly was!

Clint headed for the Antelope Hotel. He would take his chances and try to keep one step ahead of them. But if they caught up to him and that jealous sonofabitch started shooting instead of listening, then someone was going to die before the night was over.

Chapter Five

As Clint pounded down the alley, he could hear shouts and then Milly shouted, "I don't care, you don't own me yet and if you keep on like this, you never will!"

An instant later, he heard the distinctive sound of a face being slapped and he wondered if it was the sheriff's or Milly's. One thing he was sure of, their engagement would be damned rocky.

He rounded a corner and shot in between two buildings. A spider web threw its sticky mask across his face and he cussed and tore it from his eyes. If there was anything spookier than running face-first through a spider web, he'd like to know about it. Main Street was still busy and quite a few people turned to watch as he sprinted across it and beelined for the Antelope. He hit the boardwalk and shot through the door and lobby.

The desk clerk yelled something about guests not being permitted to run in this establishment but Clint paid the man no mind as he took the stairs two at a time. When he hit the second story landing, he staggered, fighting for breath and then hurried down to his room and started to grab the doorhandle. At the very last instant, he remembered his tiny matchstick and when he looked down, he saw that it had fallen.

Someone had been inside and might still be there.

24

Clint drew his gun. He could hear shouting in the street and knew he did not have time to pussyfoot around. Taking a deep breath, he twisted the doorknob, found it unlocked and threw himself inside. The room was dark except for moonlight filtering through the window. Even so, Clint saw a shadow move. He dove for the floor as gunfire stabbed yellow and a bullet cut through the air where he should have been standing. Clint fired, aiming for the man's leg.

His bullet scored and the man howled in pain and grabbed the fleshy part of his thigh. Clint was on his feet in an instant. He jumped the man and grabbed him by the collar, smashing the barrel of his sixgun against the fellow's head. The intruder grunted and dropped to the floor.

Clint wished he had time to search the man and learn if he was a deputy or a reputation seeker. But from the tie-down holster and fancy vest with pretty silver conchos, Clint would guess the latter. This hunch was strengthened when he noticed the man was holding a pearl-handled revolver with a filed-down gunsight.

Clint scowled. Quickly, he rifled through his pockets and found twenty dollars in gold. It was a small lesson to be paid in return for not being killed. Clint grabbed his own saddlebags and his Winchester rifle. He decided against taking his bedroll because he had a hunch the next fifteen minutes were going to be fast and furious. A man had to travel light to get out of the kind of scrape Milly had gotten him into tonight.

Clint dashed to the door. The intruder was groaning. Maybe that would give Clint a few extra minutes, if the sheriff might think he was the Gunsmith. Any sound in the room would make him think twice about coming through that door and possibly getting riddled.

"Keep 'em thinking," he said to the semi-conscious gunman who was already swimming up through a sea of pain. "Much obliged."

He locked the door and jumped for the stairway but skidded to a halt when he heard the desk clerk yell, "No running! Please."

"Uh-oh," he said, whirling around and pounding back down the hallway, trying two doorknobs and finding them locked. Bootsteps on the stairs told him he was out of time, so he tried a third door and when it didn't open, he gave it his shoulder just as the man inside opened it a crack. Clint's weight and momentum broke the lock and he bowled the startled occupant over as they both spilled into the room.

"Excuse me," he whispered, clamping his mouth over the bald headed man who was about to yell a warning. "I know it's rude to invite yourself in this way but sometimes a man's life takes rank over his manners. This is such a time. If you yell, I will split your head open with my gun. Do you understand?"

The man responded by biting Clint's hand, spitting and saying, "Yes, damn you."

He was short and fat and had the look of a successful businessman. He spoke with a New Yorker's accent. Clint had met a few in his time, men with ink-stained fingers always asking questions and looking for a fresh angle to an old western story. Clint turned and closed the door. He locked it and sagged against the doorjamb as he heard the sheriff yell a few doors away, "I can hear you in there, Gunsmith! Open up and throw your gun out or die, you whoring sonofabitch!"

The wounded intruder in Clint's room screamed something unintelligible. Clint closed his eyes for a moment trying to catch his breath. He would have to go through the window and drop down to the street. The sheriff would search every room and the first place he would look was under the beds. There was no place to hide in here and, anyway, the New York businessman would reveal his whereabouts at the first opportunity.

Clint turned and started for the window.

"That's just far enough, mister," the easterner hissed. "One step and you are going to headline the obituary pages of tomorrow's newspaper."

Clint froze. In the easterner's hand was one of those damn pepperbox pistols. The kind that had a nasty habit of exploding all barrels at once and chopping away everything in its path like grapeshot out of a military cannon.

"Who are you? More to the point, how much reward is there for your capture, dead or alive?"

Clint felt sweat begin to trickle down his backbone. The room was stuffy and he had no doubt that the easterner was more than ready to open him up like a can of sardines. But maybe even worse than all of that, the room had no window. He was trapped!

The easterner cocked the hammer on his gun. Clint swallowed. "You ever shoot that thing before? It's almost as dangerous to your hand as it is to my health. Better put it down so we can be reasonable men and talk this over."

"You have five seconds to live or leave this room in the prone position. Talk."

"I'm the Gunsmith."

The gun sagged a little. "Even I've heard of you. How do I know that?"

"I don't know. Most anyone would tell you. Listen to the sheriff out there!"

"Gunsmith! Open up this door and quit trying to buy time."

Clint smiled hopefully. "I guess that ought to convince you."

"All right," the easterner said, still not looking very friendly. He was about five-eight and rotund with a handlebar mustache and puffy red cheeks. His hair was streaked with gray and he had wide, sloping shoulders that suggested power beneath the blubber. His nose was crooked and Clint noticed that a few of the knuckles on his gunhand were broken. This man had been in a few fights. "Keep talking."

In as few words as possible, Clint explained the mess that Milly had gotten him into. He ended by saying, "All I want is to get out of town alive and without having to kill anyone. Can you help?"

"I might be able to. Will you take me with you and give me a few stories for my magazine?"

So, he was a reporter of some kind. Clint bit back a groan. He had never had a correct quote or met one of these types that he trusted, but then again, he was not in any bargaining position. "All right."

"Good. Undress."

"What!"

"Shhh! Keep your voice down. Undress and get into my bed. When they knock, I'll tell them that we are having a party and to stay the hell out."

"Might work," Clint mused, hating the idea but unable to think of a better one.

"It has to. And if it don't, it's your ass that'll get drilled, not mine."

Clint kicked off his boots and ignored the look he got because he wasn't even wearing socks. He shoved his boots, hat and gunbelt under the bed and then climbed in and pulled the covers up to his chin and covered his head with the pillow. He kept his sixgun in his fist. The light was very dim and this might work, but if it didn't, he was going to take a few lawmen with him. Damned if he was going to die bootless and empty-handed shaking in a reporter's bed!

Chapter Six

Clint heard the door splinter across the hallway and then two sudden gunshots. There was a terrible silence and then he heard someone curse savagely.

"We killed the wrong man, for God's sake! That ain't the Gunsmith!"

"Search every room!"

The easterner was already in his nightshirt and now he jumped into bed beside Clint and whispered, "Stay under that pillow and pretend you're asleep."

Clint ground his teeth but he did as he was told. If this didn't work, he was going to wish he was dead rather than caught this way. And if these men hadn't been lawmen, he'd have stood his ground despite the long odds.

Their door shook under the impact of fists.

"Who is it!" the easterner roared. "Can't a man get any sleep in this damned hotel!"

"It's the sheriff. Open up in the name of the law!"

The easterner got up and Clint could hear him stomping across the floor. Clint gripped his sixgun even tighter knowing that he was in a mighty sad position to defend himself. One thing sure, if he fired from under the blankets, he was going to catch the bed on fire and be in a terrible fix.

"Hurry up, we ain't got all day!"

"I'm coming!" the easterner roared, sounding madder than a caged cougar.

Clint pulled the pillow up just enough to see light flood in from the hallway as the door opened. He saw a tall man with a badge and a gun in his fist flanked by his deputies.

"What is the meaning of this outrage!" the easterner demanded.

"My name is Sheriff Wilson and these men are deputies. We have a fugitive of the law up here on this landing and we mean to find him."

"Well he isn't in here! Me and . . ." the easterner cleared his voice and forced embarrassment into it. "Listen, Sheriff, the lady with me is . . . well, it would cause her some . . ."

The sheriff craned his neck to see better. "Who is she?"

"I'd rather not say," the easterner wheedled.

"Then I'll have to come in and. . . ."

"All right. All right! But for your ears alone. Do you swear that her identity will remain nameless?"

The sheriff nodded eagerly. He motioned his men away and then the easterner whispered something in his ear.

Clint could clearly see the astonishment reflected on the lawman's face.

"Well, I never thought Mrs.—"

"Shhh! Please, the lady would be ruined in Tucson if this scandal got out."

"Damn right she would," the sheriff said, with a shake of his head. "No wonder she covered her face with that pillow. It is a hell of a thing when—"

"Sheriff, please! May I close the door and bolt it for our own safety?"

"Yeah, you'd better do that. Because when me and the boys find the Gunsmith, I'll shoot first and talk later."

"What did the man do?"

"Never mind, goddammit! You got your secrets, we've got our own."

"I see. Good hunting, Sheriff."

The door shut and Clint tossed the pillow to the floor and jumped out of bed. He pulled his boots on and then retrieved his gunbelt and Stetson. This entire episode was one he would just as soon forget but as another door crashed open down the hallway and he heard angry shouts, Clint knew that he owed the easterner a debt.

"I'm much obliged to you," he said, sticking out his hand. "What is your name?"

"Harold Westerfield. I'm sure you've heard of me. *New York Gentleman's Quarterly.*"

Clint frowned. "I don't have the chance to read New York magazines very often, Harold. But I'm sure you're a fine writer and I'm grateful to you for getting me out of this fix. That sheriff is pure crazy with jealousy and I wish Milly had told the truth of things. Anyway, thanks. It's been . . ."

"Wait just a damn minute," Harold bristled. "We had a deal! I agreed to help you in return for your agreement to give me a couple of interviews."

Clint could hear another door being assaulted by the sheriff and his men. It would give any minute and when it did and the lawman hurled inside, Clint intended to hit the stairway and keep moving.

"Gunsmith? Are you or are you not a gentleman who honors his agreements?" Harold Westerfield demanded.

Clint frowned, trying not to let his temper get the best of him. "Listen to them, Harold! I either have to make a run for it, or take them on in a gunfight. I haven't got time to give you an interview right now. They might come back here and want to look under the bed or something. So, I'm leaving and if you want an interview, we'll just have to do it another time."

"Where and when?"

"I don't know! Can't we. . . ."

"I'm coming with you!" the easterner said, grabbing his bag and stuffing his clothes and belongings inside.

Clint heard the hinges starting to tear loose from the door. "Hurry up!"

When Clint heard the door finally break loose under the force of the lawmen, he opened Harold's door and headed for the stairs. If Harold was coming along, then he'd have to keep up or be left behind. It wasn't the easterner's hide that the Sheriff and his men were after tonight!

Clint raced down the stairs and shot across the lobby hearing the hotel clerk shriek an alarm to the men upstairs. Clint would have liked to have flattened the blabbermouth but there simply was no time. He collided with a man in the doorway and sent him cussing and sprawling. Then, Clint was racing for the livery stable. He passed the Blue Dog Saloon and when he came to an intersection, he glanced back to see if the sheriff and his deputies were already on his tail. They weren't, but Harold Westerfield was and he looked anything but pleased. The man had pulled on his trousers but hadn't had the time to tuck his nightshirt into them or even to put on his shoes. He was carrying a suitcase in each hand and his short, stubby legs were pistoning him forward with surprising speed.

Clint did not know whether to laugh or to get mad. He sure did wish the guy would give up but that did not seem to be his nature. Well, Clint thought, I'll give it to him for being stubborn, but he's still going to have to keep up until I'm safely out of Tucson.

The livery was locked up tight and Clint had to bang a pitchfork over and over against the barn door to get the liveryman to open up.

"What the hell time of night is it?" the man asked sleepily.

Clint pushed inside and it was pitch dark. "Got a lantern?"

"Sure but. . . ."

"Then light it," Clint ordered. "I need to saddle Duke and get out of here right now."

"Did you rob a bank or something?" The liveryman took a backstep. He seemed wide awake now. "Say, listen, if you're in trouble with the law, I don't want to be a part of whatever you got into."

"Fine," Clint said, gritting his teeth. "Light a lantern and go back to bed. All I want is to leave in a hurry."

"Hey wait!" Harold Westerfield cried hoarsely. "Goddamn you, Gunsmith! We have a deal and you're not getting wriggling out of it!"

The liveryman stared at the easterner and said, "I don't even want to know what that feller did to make him come runnin' down the street half dressed. I'll get a lantern and then you and him are on your own."

"Harold, you own a horse and tack?"

The man was breathing so hard that he just shook his head.

When the liveryman brought the lantern, Clint took it and stepped inside lighting it. He peered back into the street but saw no pursuit. "We need to buy a horse, saddle, bridle and blankets."

The liveryman blinked, then a slow smile spread across his face. "And you need them real fast, that right? And with no questions asked."

"Something like that," Clint said, knowing what was coming next. "Got to be a damn good horse. Fast and with stamina enough to stay with my black."

"Few animals alive could do that but I got one that won't slow you too much. Roan gelding in the stall next to yours. I will sell him and the tack you need for two hundred dollars cash."

"What!" Harold yelled. "That is robbery! I refuse to pay it!"

The liveryman just shrugged. "Suit yourselves. Me, I'm going back to bed."

Harold grabbed him by the arm and spun him around. The liveryman threw a punch but Harold blocked it, ducked and drove his fist into the livery-man's stomach hard enough to lift him off his feet, then drop him to his knees.

"I'm sorry," Harold said, sounding like he actually meant it. "But my publisher's budget doesn't permit undue extravagances. I will pay you one hundred and fifty dollars cash for the horse and its trappings. Is that acceptable?"

"Ye . . . yes!" the liveryman choked, trying to get his wind. "But you . . . you're going to saddle the sonofabitch!"

Clint saw the easterner count out the money and shove it into the liveryman's shirt pocket. It was twice what a good horse and outfit was worth but under the circumstances, fair. Clint saddled and bridled both horses as fast as he could. He had to help the fat east-erner into the saddle. The roan was a big, strong horse like Duke which was very fortunate because an eight-hundred pounder could not have carried such weight without tiring quickly.

"Aren't my stirrups too long!" Harold cussed, still furious because he realized he was going to have to leave his suitcases here and that the liveryman would prob-ably sell them without his permission.

Clint looked at the stirrups. The soles of the east-erner's shoes could barely reach them. It was obvious that Harold Westerfield had never ridden before in his life, and Clint could not help but suppress a smile. So far, Harold hadn't suffered any real indignities, but now Clint would see what kind of stuff the man was made of.

"They're short enough," Clint said. "Let's ride!"

The liveryman held up his lantern and hollered, "Go

out the back way and circle the corrals. Follow around behind the manure pile and then cut south toward Mexico. If the sheriff comes, I'll tell him you went west."

"Much obliged."

"I'll bet you killed a bunch of men tonight, didn't you Gunsmith!" the liveryman yelled, sounding as if he hoped it were true.

Clint leaped into the saddle and reined Duke. "Not yet," he answered as he and his horse blasted out into the stableyard, circled the corrals and manure pile, then headed into the moonlight. He raced down a backstreet and set the dogs to barking and chasing after them. When he glanced over his shoulder, Harold Westerfield was hanging onto the saddlehorn for all he was worth.

Clint looked up at the warm desert sky. The stars were brilliantly clear. He slowed Duke to a trot and heard the easterner yell something that was not very complimentary.

Clint chuckled softly to himself. The magazine writer had persistence and courage, that was for sure. He might even be fun to ride the trail with a few miles.

Chapter Seven

"Stop!" Harold Westerfield screeched.

Clint pulled Duke to a halt and twisted around in the saddle. Harold was in agony. He was bent over his saddlehorn and even in the poor light, Clint could see the man's face was pale. "What happened?" he asked with genuine concern.

"I bounced so high I landed on the horn," the man gasp. "I can't gallop any farther!"

Clint frowned. "Well, we can't stop here. You're going to have to keep up or return to Tucson."

The man managed to raise his head. "No gentleman would do that to another. A deal is a deal!"

"I never said anything about being a gentleman. And if that's a necessary requirement for being interviewed by your magazine, then I'll say adios right here and now."

Harold drew a deep and ragged breath. "It isn't. Gentlemen like to read about scoundrels. You are eminently qualified on the latter count."

Clint smiled. "No sense getting nasty just because you busted your balls over the horn, Harold. I guess I do owe you an interview and if you feel up to it, ask away."

The man straightened a little in his saddle. "I am without both pen and paper and I need some time. This isn't the place. Where are you headed?''

"I haven't decided. Maybe the Colorado Rockies. Maybe down toward Santa Fe. Somewhere I can find relief from this heat and maybe even wet a fishing line. I like to relax in summer.''

"I see. Let me tell you where I think we should head for right now. A place that will fit your requirements and give us a little time to get acquainted. A place where we will be treated very well, expected to do nothing, waited upon hand and foot and fed like kings.''

"I can't afford it.''

"It's free,'' Harold said with a smug, but pained grin. "Interested?''

"I'd have to be a fool to say no.''

"Then listen to me,'' Harold said. "I am out west on a magazine assignment covering new and undiscovered western resorts. My editors want small but rustic places. Resorts with charm where you are well fed, well taken care of and might even meet some real cowboys. Phony dude ranches are springing up all over the place and many of them are just revolving doors where easterners are treated like so many dumb, pedigreed cattle.''

"Go on,'' Clint said, more than a little interested.

"Well, I have a line on a very rustic and new resort less than two hundred miles east of here. It's up on the Mogollon Rim. Elevation around eleven thousand feet so the nights are cool and the days never get above seventy five degrees.''

"I've heard that's pretty country.''

"I've heard it's spectacular country,'' Harold said. "My editors received a glowing letter from a woman named Dinah Morgan. She told us that she has just opened a new resort and that it will become the finest in the west. Morgan described a beautiful lake and she did happen to say that the fishing was so good you could almost scoop the trout out of the water with your hat.''

"Is that a fact?''

"Yes it is, Gunsmith. And the best part is that Dinah Morgan agreed to let us stay for free just to get the publicity. After a couple of weeks, we leave and I have several other resorts that I am supposed to visit before autumn. You'll never get a chance like this again, I swear it."

Clint nodded. It did sound great but there were some serious questions first. "That's perfect for you, Harold, but what about me? Why should someone like this Morgan woman let me have a free vacation?"

"We'll tell her that you are my assistant and the magazine's photographer."

"But I don't know anything about photography! Besides, won't it look strange that I don't even have a camera?"

"Not at all. We can say that it was lost on the way out from New York and you are hoping to receive it or a replacement."

Clint rubbed his jaw. "Doesn't seem quite right to take advantage under false pretenses."

"Listen, the publicity the *New York Gentleman's Quarterly* can give them is priceless! Next summer they will be overrun with high paying guests if I write favorably about their resort. I can make—or break—them."

Harold patted his stomach. "In the past seven weeks I have put on forty pounds because of the steaks, the pies, the wonderful cooking that they give you at these resorts. And being anxious to have a good write-up, the owners will make it a point that we're treated even better than the paying guests. Quite frankly, Gunsmith, you look a little lean and wolfish. A few weeks of rest, fishing and good food would do a wonder for you."

"I have been riding and eating a little on the thin side these past few months," Clint admitted.

"Then how about it? Accept and we both win. You get the vacation of your life and I get enough gunfighter stories and information to write a book if I ever chose to. But I won't. No, instead, I'll write some articles and sell them to my editors for a bonus—or maybe a promotion to chief of publishing."

Clint nodded. "I have nothing better to do. All right, it's a deal. But I don't think I'll be able to fool the Morgan woman very long. She didn't say anything about two guests, did she?"

"No, but. . . ."

"Tell you what, Harold. Let's ride into Phoenix and buy a cheap old camera. I don't even need any film. Just so I have something to go through the motions with."

Harold stuck out his hand. "Agreed. As long as I don't have to buy it. I'm afraid this damned horse and saddle cost me two weeks of my travel expense money."

"It's a good horse. Besides, you just said that the interviews I give you will make you the chief of publishing. So you'll soon get a big promotion and a raise. Don't let a little thing like buying me a camera stand in your way of success, Harold."

The easterner grinned. "Gunsmith, you're a clever man—and well spoken. I think we're going to have a good time together this summer."

"Where do we go after Piney?"

"A place called Flagstaff. Supposed to be real nice too."

"I've heard the same." Clint felt good. It was funny, he thought, as they moved out again in the direction of Phoenix, how a fella's luck could change so fast. An hour ago he figured he was going to have to kill or be killed by six lawmen. That was bad luck to have been deceived by a woman as pretty and hungry as Milly. Worse luck yet to discover her fiance was a jealous sheriff with sawdust instead of brains. But this meeting up with Harold Westerfield, now that was good luck for certain.

"Don't trot, please," Harold groaned.

Clint pulled Duke back to a walk. "Sorry," he said,

thinking as how traveling this slow to Phoenix and then up to Piney was going to tax his patience considerably. But he had no doubts at all that it would be well worth the wait.

"Say Harold?"

"Yeah?"

"How old do you suppose this Dinah Morgan woman is?"

"I've no idea."

"Miss or Mrs.?"

"Miss, Gunsmith. But you had better watch yourself this time. I don't want a repeat of tonight's performance."

"Not a chance, Harold." They rode side by side across the desert for a long time. A horned owl silently plunged out of the sky and disappeared into the brush. They heard a hard flutter of wings on earth and then a dying screech. Both men saw the owl carry a twitching rabbit aloft as its great, silent wings beat their way across the moon.

"One other thing, Harold."

"Yeah?"

"Back there in the Antelope Hotel. You told that Sheriff Wilson you were sleeping with a married woman. Someone important in Tucson. Who was she?"

"Preacher's wife."

Clint stared. "Well, why'd you do a miserable thing like that?"

"Preachers are always standing on the pulpit and giving other people hell, sometimes it's a good idea to give them a little back. Huh?"

"You are a real pisser, Harold. Got a mean streak half as wide as your already tender backside."

That caused Harold to laugh right out loud. "You better not forget that either, Gunsmith. I may be a gentleman, but that doesn't mean I'm a sucker. I'd have shot you dead back there in my room if you'd have made the wrong move.''

The smile on Clint's lips evaporated. There was no sense in telling Harold that he could have drawn and fired so quickly that they would both have died in that hotel room. Just like he had told the two boys in the cafe: It was better not to let those you did not completely trust to see all the cards you were holding.

Clint took in a deep breath of the sage-scented night air and thought ahead to a cool mountain lake and the big, splashing trout he would catch. It was going to be real nice even if he did have to pretend to be Harold's assistant and magazine photographer. Especially if Dinah Morgan was young and pretty.

Chapter Eight

Harold Westerfield was not in a good mood. They had been forced to pay one hundred and seventy dollars for a monstrous box camera and the necessary glass negatives, chemicals and other necessary paraphernalia. The whole works weighed over two hundred pounds so Harold had been forced to buy a pack mule and saddle to carry it all costing him another sixty dollars which he did not have. This lack of cash forced Harold to send two telegrams to New York City requesting additional expense money.

New York had not been pleased and a flurry of embarrassing telegrams had traveled back and forth demanding further explanation concerning the need for a mule, pack saddle and additional supplies. The affair had taken one entire afternoon and Harold had been outraged by his publisher's stinginess and insulting lack of trust.

"My publisher and his stockholders are worth a fortune! One that I helped create," he had raged. "And here they are niggling and badgering me over a lousy couple of hundred dollars! Outrageous treatment for a man of my professional reputation."

Clint had not gotten himself embroiled in the haggling over expense money. Instead, he had tried to listen very patiently to the photographer who had sold them the camera. Gone were the days of the daguerrotype system, which had been fragile and unreproducible and required metal plates to catch and hold the photograph images. Now, the newer wet-plate collodian and glass negative system allowed as many prints as were needed to be reproduced on paper. But there were still many drawbacks, including the fact that you had to chemically develop the picture immediately in absolute darkness—a tricky process that the Gunsmith had to try four times even to begin to master.

Now, as they followed the Salt River out of Phoenix into the Mazatzal Mountains and the Mogollon Rim, Clint still was not sure if he remembered all the steps in the chemical process. Clint knew how furious Harold would become if he failed to create anything the *New York Gentleman's Quarterly* could use and print.

The hell with it, Clint thought, I am a gunsmith and I was a top-notch lawman but I haven't the knowledge or the patience to be a photographer.

"You had better remember how to do it," Harold grumped as if reading the Gunsmith's mind. "I intend to get my investment back in the sale of pictures you take."

Clint said nothing. The road up into the mountains was steep and there were many switchbacks. From Phoenix, the mountains had looked desolate and sterile, but once you began to climb up into them, they seemed to change. They were still pretty dry at the lower levels, but there were springs and plenty of water. Clint saw deer and even a band of wild sheep in the distance. The roan was having a hard time carrying Harold's weight up such a steep grade and Clint had to stop often and let it catch its breath and rest until its overtaxed muscles stopped twitching.

"Maybe you ought to stay away from the feed bag a little more this time," Clint suggested.

"Go to hell," the writer grunted. "When this assignment is over, then I'll go on a diet. Not until."

Clint studied the gasping, trembling roan. "That isn't going to help him now. If I'd have realized we were going up a mountain like this, I would have suggested a draft animal to carry you."

Harold shot him a go-to-hell look that amused Clint. It was fun to prod this man now and then.

They camped overnight on the face of the mountain and, for the first time in weeks, the air cooled down into the sixties. Clint thought it felt wonderful. He bathed in a cold stream and then sat in his shorts and watched the sun go down and the stars come up. The soft gurgle of the stream close by his bedroll sounded like music and he awoke the next morning feeling revitalized.

The next two days, they climbed even higher. Then they were on the Mogollon Rim and the air was crisp and smelling of pine trees. Ahead of them lay a long meadow of deep grass and Clint grinned as he patted Duke's powerful shoulder. "It's lunchtime for you, old man."

He stepped down, unsaddled the horse, then removed the bridle and reins.

"Won't he run off!" Harold asked with alarm.

"Nope," Clint replied. "He knows I need him and so he'll stick around. But I'd recommend that we hobble the roan and the mule or they'll head on back to Phoenix for sure."

"We aren't stopping for long, are we?"

"Couple of hours," Clint said, stretching out and pulling his Stetson over his eyes. "Long enough for the horses to fill their bellies on this sweet grass and for me to take a siesta."

"Well, for hell's sake! Piney might just be a few miles up ahead. Why stay here when we can stretch out on a feather bed at the Morgan woman's resort?"

Clint thumbed his hat back and frowned. "If you're in such an all-fired hurry, then you might as well ride on ahead. Me, I'm letting my horse get his fill while I take a nap. Don't worry, I'll catch up to you before dark. No problem."

Harold didn't miss the obvious reference to the fact that he was responsible for the slow pace they had been traveling. He felt insulted. "Well I may just do that, by damned!"

"Suit yourself."

Clint pulled his hat back over his eyes and forgot about Harold Westerfield. He smelled grass and wild-flowers. Less than sixty miles down on the desert floor the temperature in Phoenix would be hot enough to boil your brain pan. But up here, paradise.

Clint fell asleep with a smile of contentment on his lips.

He awoke with a start and with that innate gun-fighter's sense of alarm that had saved his life many times in the past. For a moment, he lay perfectly still listening for some sound that did not belong. If there was danger very close, he wanted to pretend that he was asleep and thus gain the advantage of surprise. But he heard nothing and, just as he was about to push his hat back from his eyes, he realized that he should have heard many things: the contented chomping of Duke's big teeth as he chewed grass, the stomping of Duke's hoof or swish of his tail as an occasional fly bothered to land on his sleek coat.

The raucous cries of a blue-jay, the chattering of a squirrel from the bough of a pine tree. But the meadow was silent, and that was the alarm that had warned him of danger.

Clint's senses sharped and he slowly began to edge his hand down his side to his gun.

"Touch it and you are in serious trouble, mister," the voice said from very near. "Just lie still and keep your hat over your eyes until I say so."

Clint heard the ominous cocking of a sixgun and he knew that he would have no chance at all if he tried to draw while lying on his back. He felt his own gun being eased out of his holster and then the man said, "All right, mister, you can sit up now real slow, hands out from your sides."

Clint sat realizing that he had slept too long and there were three cowmen with drawn guns staring down at him.

"Who are you, stranger?"

"My name is Clint and . . . and I work for a newspaper writer named Harold Westerfield. I'm his photographer and assistant."

"Bullshit! We've already had a little talk with Mr. Westerfield."

Clint had no idea what Harold might have said but decided he had no choice but to stick to their agreed-upon story. "Then the man told you the same as I just did. You must have seen my camera and gear."

"If you worked for him," the tallest one said contemptuously, "how come you're taking a long siesta and he's sashaying off through the forest?"

"I got tired," Clint said lamely as he pushed himself to his feet. He was in no mood for this kind of nonsense and wanted to know why he was being held at gunpoint. "So what the hell are you doing with guns in your hands?"

"I ask the questions," the leader said. He was broad shouldered, late twenties with blonde hair and ice-blue eyes. He was very tall and quite good looking except for a straggly mustache. "My name is Johnny Bolt and these boys work for me and my father. We own this grass your horse is chewing."

Clint bristled. "Well let me pay you two bits and I'll be on my way."

"Stay put." Johnny Bolt nodded to one of his men

who nodded back and then went to catch Duke.

Clint wanted to protest but the gun stopped him. "Is your ranch in the habit of stealing cowhorses, or what?" he said tightly.

"No, but maybe you are. You got a bill of sale for that fine animal?"

"Yeah. It's in my saddlebags."

"Arnie, take a look."

Clint watched Arnie trudge over to the saddlebags and open them. He rummaged around and finally found the paper but he obviously could not read.

"Give it to me, Arnie." Johnny Bolt read the bill of sale twice before he reluctantly nodded. "Looks legal."

"Is legal," Clint said through clenched teeth. "Now, why don't you put those guns away before I start to lose my temper."

"You don't sound like a photographer or any assistant to me," Johnny said, his gun not moving an inch from Clint's chest. "Maybe if you're not a horse thief, you're a cattle rustler. Arnie?"

"Yeah?"

"You find a runnin' iron in those saddle bags?"

"Afraid not, Boss."

Clint grinned wickedly. "You got any more ridiculous charges you can't back up?"

"Just one, mister. This is Bolt Ranch land you are on and it's like I told your fat friend. Nobody trespasses on my father's ranch. Nobody. Especially someone come up from the city to write some kind of cock and bull story about Dinah's Place. We don't like strangers up here on the Rim, and especially strangers who might invite a bunch of rich eastern dudes."

"You and your father own this whole mountain range, do you, Johnny?"

"Enough of it."

"But not all," Clint said pointedly. "Listen, this is a

free country and I'll get off your land if you tell me where it ends but then you don't tell me or anyone else a damned thing.''

Johnny's face went white with anger. "Maybe I ought to teach you a lesson, mister. And when I'm finished, you're going to tell me who you really are.''

"Are you going to teach me with or without your gun, brave man?''

"I never beat anyone except in a fair, stand-up fight,'' Johnny said as he holstered his gun. When Johnny raised his big fists, there was a glint in his eye that told him this rancher's son was no coward and no slouch in a fight. He looked strong as a horse, five or six years younger than the Gunsmith, and twenty pounds heavier. Even so, Clint figured he had at least goaded the man into giving him some kind of a fighting chance.

And that was usually all the Gunsmith ever needed.

Chapter Nine

Johnny lunged, his fist a blur as it swept toward Clint's face. Clint ducked the blow and slammed his own fist into Johnny's ribs. The man grunted in pain but when Clint tried to catch him with an overhand right, Johnny danced back out of range and said, "All right, so you know how to fight a little. Let's see how good you really are."

They began to circle each other warily. Johnny was smiling and when Clint feinted with a left and then stabbed with the right, the rancher's son countered with blinding speed. One minute he was dancing around, and the next he was driving two quick jabs to Clint's eyes and following with a whacking good overhand that dropped him like a heavy stone.

"Get up," Johnny said with a grin. "This boxing lesson isn't half over yet."

Clint got up and brushed the dirt from the seat of his pants. One side of his face was numb and he could feel his eye swelling. If he didn't know better, he would have thought that Johnny was wearing brass knuckles. "Where did you learn to fight like that?" he gritted, circling again.

"Harvard boxing club." Johnny jabbed him again only this time the blow landed on Clint's nose and made his eyes smart and water. "Class of '72."

49

"I'm impressed," Clint said, ducking another punch and then unleashing a short but powerful blow back to those same ribs. Johnny grunted, then he reached out and grabbed on to keep Clint from pounding him in the side again.

They strained against each other and Clint managed to hook a spur behind Johnny's leg and topple him. They went down tearing at each other, punching, driving elbows and fists at throats and faces. One minute Clint was on top, the next Johnny Bolt. When they finally clawed to their feet again, Clint got in one more bone-crunching punch to those same tender ribs.

Johnny's face paled and now he stood bent a little at the waist. Clint used that as an indication that he had at least cracked one of the man's ribs. It gave him renewed confidence and he moved in, taking a stiff right to deliver two more blows, one a sweeping uppercut to the solar plexis that send Johnny backpeddling.

"Come on, Boss!" Arnie yelled, "don't let the bastard hit you in the body no more. Keep him away! Better yet, let me tear his arms off for you."

Clint glanced sideways at the man. Arnie was a scarred bruiser of a man. A slab of gristle and bone, all muscle between the ears and no brain.

"Stay out of this Arnie," Johnny Bolt hissed. "It's my fight—win or lose!" He shot a left jaw with some steam on it.

Clint ducked and feinted with another uppercut. Johnny stepped back but Clint had been expecting it and now he launched himself at the rancher and caught the man moving away with a looping right overhand blow that wasn't pretty but sent Johnny sprawling. It was an off-balance punch but it had had everything that Clint owned behind it. Johnny landed flat on his back and his breath whooshed out of his lungs. But just when Clint was sure the fight was over, Johnny Bolt rolled to his knees and wobbled to his feet. Clint waited for the man to stand and then he attacked with a vengeance. Three thundering punches sent the young rancher crashing back down and the man lay there groaning, and then he started to climb back to his feet.

"Stay down," Clint warned, almost pleaded. "You've nothing to be ashamed about. You're whipped."

But Johnny shook his head trying to clear the glaze from his eyes. "Don't like to lose," he muttered drunkenly.

He dove for Clint's knees but his strength and speed were gone and the Gunsmith had no trouble leaping out of his grasp. "You've had enough!"

"No!" Johnny shouted hoarsely, his gaze swinging past Clint. "Arnie, don't. . . ."

That was all Clint heard as he started to turn and glimpsed the metallic glint of a gunbarrel arcing through the sky. It struck him across the forehead so hard he dropped into a black hole and just kept falling.

"Wake up, Clint."

Clint felt his head being rolled from side to side and his cheeks being squeezed by a powerful thumb and forefinger. He opened his eyes and saw a red haze and somewhere behind that, he saw and heard Harold Westerfield.

"Leave me alone," he wheezed.

"I can't," the easterner said roughly. "If we don't get off the Bolt Ranch by dawn, they'll be back and this time, they might use bullets instead of gun barrels on you."

Clint felt himself being lifted to his feet. His legs felt like wooden stumps and his knees kept bending like well-oiled hinges. He felt as if he had been stampeded over by a herd of buffalo.

"Grab the saddlehorn and hang on when I lift you," Harold ordered.

Before Clint quite realized it, he was being hoisted up and over the saddle. For a moment, he tottered drunkenly and almost toppled over the far side but he held on and managed to stay erect.

Harold used a rope to tie him between the cantle and the saddlehorn. "Somebody really busted you hard across the skull, Clint. Hard enough to make you bleed from the ears."

Clint tried to focus on the words and understand what Harold was telling him. "The ears?"

"Yes. I seen enough fights and head injuries to know you got what is called a brain concussion. It'll probably be all right after a few days or weeks of rest, but you need to be kept flat and get plenty of rest."

Clint nodded but even that slight motion of his head caused a violent red flash to fire across the backs of his eyeballs. "I'll kill that Arnie," he groaned.

"Arnie. Didn't Johnny Bolt do this?"

"No. It was a good fight but he was whipped." Clint remembered how Bolt had even tried to shout a warning. Maybe the man had some sense of decency in him after all. Probably the result of his Harvard days in the boxing club.

"Well, it doesn't matter who did it," Harold said. "It took me almost all night to find you out here and it'll be dawn in a few hours. We have to get to Piney."

"How far?"

"They told me it was fifteen miles across some rough mountain trails. It's going to be damned hard on you, Clint. I wish there was some other way to do this, but there isn't. I'd be afraid to leave you again."

"Lead on," Clint said tightly. "But don't expect me to carry on a civil conversation."

Harold mounted the roan and grabbed Duke's reins. There was no mule in sight. "Where'd he go?" Clint asked.

"They run him off into the forest. Last I seen of the

bastard he was tearing the camera and tripod to pieces against the trees. Pack, camera, tripod and chemicals were flying in every damn direction. Including the stupid mule, that's about three hundred dollars shot to hell, Clint. I'm going to be as eager as you to even the score. But I think we had better swear out a warrant for Bolt's arrest and let the law take the matter up.''

If it wouldn't have hurt so bad, Clint would have laughed outright. Harold showed what a dude he really was by thinking that the law would help them. Unless he was way off base, Clint figured that the Bolts probably had things pretty much their own way up here in the Mogollon Rim country of Arizona. They no doubt supported a lot of the towns and that meant their business supported the sheriff too.

Clint reckoned that was a pessimistic view of how the law in a small town operated, but it was a fact of life. If Harold Westerfield thought that anyone except the two of them was going to settle the score, he was in for a big disappointment. But it hurt too much to explain all that, so Clint just hung on tight and let Duke carry him to the nearest doctor.

There would come a day of reckoning, but that day was definitely in the future. Until then, he would have to rest and get his strength back. But not in a crackerbox hotel, Clint had it in his mind that he would get the best care possible at the resort.

I'm a lucky man, he thought, that this happened just before I am getting ready to start the best vacation of my life.

Chapter Ten

Clint could hear Harold shouting from inside the hotel. "What do you mean you don't want to give us a room for the night and that no doctor will get involved! There's a man outside on horseback with a concussion, for Chrissakes!"

Clint heard a pleading, and then the slamming of the hotel door hard enough to send one huge pane of window glass shattering back into the hotel lobby.

"I can't believe this!" Harold yelled. "Is everyone in this three horse town afraid of the Bolts!"

Clint was at least able to sit upright without being tied in the saddle anymore. "Let's go find that Morgan woman and start living the life of ease," he croaked, trying to fight off the pounding in his skull. "I can't sit in this saddle much longer."

"You shouldn't have to! Let's hunt up the sheriff and . . ."

"No!" Clint winced in pain from the shout. He added quietly, "The sheriff isn't going to do anything and I damn sure don't want to waste anymore time fooling around. Let's find that damned resort and get me to a bed!"

His own anger doused that of the easterner. "Sorry," Harold said grudgingly. "Of course, you're right. I'll get directions. In her letter, Miss Morgan said that it

54

was only a few miles from this town."

Clint gripped the saddlehorn and waited patiently. He knew he looked like hell. His only consolation was that Johnny Bolt would be looking almost as bad and that the rancher would be riding a bed himself for awhile with a broken or cracked set of ribs.

"Got it," Harold said, coming back and crawling heavily into the saddle. "It's just about five miles down the road. They said we can't miss it if we turn off at the river and follow it another two miles to Mirror Lake. Man said there are people going out to Dinah's Place all the time and he guesses that the food must be pretty good or Dinah wouldn't be doing so well."

If he had hoped to cheer Clint up, it wasn't to be, for the Gunsmith could only whisper, "Seven miles?"

Clint groaned with dread. He was not sure that he could make it. He had about spent all of his reserves and he was having bouts of dizziness that made it hard to stay upright in the saddle.

But there seemed to be little choice so he let Harold lead Duke back down the little main street of town to the road. Somewhere before the river, Clint's head began to spin so violently that he crashed despite the ropes that bound him to the saddle. He wished he could have lost consciousness and woke up in a bed but he didn't. Instead, he had to face the indignity of having himself draped across the saddle like a dead man. He closed his eyes and when the blood all rushed to his head, Clint felt a pressure build then quickly explode in his head. He passed out.

The woman was saying, "Everyone, please! We need help to get this man to bed. Dr. Ettinger, hurry!"

Clint felt himself being pulled off the horse and then carried into a room where his boots were removed. He was placed on a bed and covered warmly though he felt hot and his skin was clammy.

A dry, white thumb lifted his eyelids one at a time. Clint wanted to bat the hand away but when he tried, he found that his arm was made of cement and it had already dried fast to the bedcovers. He stared up at the elderly doctor and guessed that the man had been retired for a few years.

He was sure of it when Dr. Ettinger said, "This man has suffered a very serious blow to the skull. He has a concussion."

"Even I knew that," Harold growled. "What do we do for him?"

"Nothing. Complete bed rest is what he needs."

"For how long?"

"A month."

Harold swore under his breath then said, "We can't stay that long! I've got three other resorts to visit and write about before the summer is over."

The woman's face swam into Clint's vision again.

She was in her early thirties, her hair was black and her face the color of ivory, the skin so perfect that it was almost transparent at the temples so that you could faintly see the blue of veins. Her eyes were large and widely spaced. Her nose was thin and straight, her lips full and moist. Clint thought her lovely. Very angelic.

"I will see that he is taken care of, Dr. Ettinger," the woman said with a dutiful sigh. "And you also, Mr. Westerfield. As long as is necessary and at no charge whatsoever. We are honored to have you for our guests and will make every effort to see that you are kept occupied."

Ettinger chuckled. "She means that you are expected to earn your own board and keep," he said winking.

"What!"

Dinah Morgan turned her cool, innocent eyes on Harold and said, "This is a 'working' ranch, sir. One in which every guest is expected to participate and help defray costs. You will also be expected to take your turn cooking, cleaning and rounding up cattle."

"By God you must be out of your mind!"

Clint actually managed a thin smile. It would do old Harold a world of good to have to earn his own keep. He would probably lose some of that blubber and exercise could not help but to mightily improve his irascible disposition.

"Mr. Westerfield," Dinah was saying, her face brittle with a smile. "I am afraid there has been some misunderstanding. I specifically mentioned in my letter that this was an authentic working ranch, not some phony convalescent home with a children's pony and a guitar player to interrupt games of checkers and dominoes."

"She's right," Dr. Ettinger said, "everyone works hard and, quite frankly, we love it. All of us! There is nothing more fun than arising in the morning with some purpose in mind. Some chores to complete, so. . . ."

"Oh shut up!" Harold raged. "I didn't come here to lift even one finger. I came to be waited upon and. . . ."

Dinah clucked her tongue twice. "Dear," she said with cocked eyebrows. "Now, I am very sure that there has been a serious misunderstanding. And I apologize. But rules are rules and I cannot let you lounge around here like a sloth while others labor for their keep."

"A sloth! How dare you!"

Some of the guests began shouting at Harold and it sounded like there was a great crowd of them. They were quite obviously loyal to Miss Morgan and her resort philosophy. Clint felt a deep peace overcome him. He would not have minded working for his board and keep at all, but the very fact that Harold minded a whole lot made this all the more fun—especially, the Gunsmith thought, since I won't be expected to lift a finger.

They were still raging at each other. When Clint had

heard enough, he groaned loudly and that silenced the argument.

"Oh, look!" Miss Morgan exclaimed. "Here we are fighting like cats and dogs while this poor photographer is almost dying of pain!"

She leaned close to him, bosom well-rounded and inviting. Clint resisted the impulse to try again to lift his hand and caress her because he was sure that would have killed her sympathy. "Is there anything that I can get you?" she whispered.

"Whiskey."

"Oh, no!" Dr. Ettinger said quickly, shaking his bony old head back and forth. "No alcohol, none at all. That would be very bad for his brain."

Clint frowned and hoped it was not very long before this old fool left.

"Then I shall be very careful about that," Miss Morgan said firmly.

Harold chuckled almost obscenely. "Hear that, old friend. Nothing to drink for you. Not a thing alcoholic!"

"Shut up," Clint whispered when Miss Morgan turned away a moment to supervise. But when she returned her attention to him, he smiled gallantly and said, "Thank you for saving my life, Ma'am."

"Oh, I am not to be thanked at all. Not yet, at least. Wait until the month is up and you are feeling normal again. Then perhaps you can think of a nice way to thank me."

Clint nodded weakly. He stared up at her lovely face and he just knew he could already think of a lot of ways to thank this woman.

Chapter Eleven

Clint awoke the following morning feeling much better. His head still throbbed mightily, but the dizziness was gone and all that was left was a constant ringing in his ears which Dr. Ettinger said might last for quite some time. Clint lay in bed studying his surroundings and found them to his liking. His was a small, one-room cabin. The double bed he lay upon had a soft feather mattress and quilted comforters. Beside him was a dresser and bedside table, both of quality construction. There were several good original paintings on the walls. One was of a beautiful lake and Clint wondered if it was the one just outside. In one corner was a small potbellied stove and in another was a coat rack and an easy chair with a table and lamp for reading. A deerskin rug and a Mexican water pitcher and wash basin completed the furnishings. All and all, Clint decided the room was pretty nice.

He eased himself out of the bed and when he sat up, a sharp pain stabbed into the back of his eyes. He groaned, but was determined to move across the cabin to the window where the curtains were pulled close. A man did not like to lie alone in a darkened room all day while the sun was shining.

Clint found his legs were steady but for some strange reason, he swayed drunkenly when he crossed the floor.

He pulled the windows open just as there was a warning call at his door and then it opened.

"Clint! What are you doing out of bed!"

He gulped, smiled and said, "Just needed a little light is all, Miss Dinah."

"Dr. Ettinger said you were to stay flat on your back for the next few days and not to be up and moving about for at least two full weeks."

"If we listened to doctors and all of us did what they ordered, we'd spend half our lives in bed expecting someone else to do the work. Isn't that right?"

"Yes, yes it is." She laughed and it had a good, happy sound to it. She was even prettier than he had remembered and her perfume filled the cabin. "But I won't allow someone sent all the way from New York to have a relapse."

She helped him back to bed and Clint felt obliged to set the record at least partially straight. "Actually," he said, "I'm not really from New York at all."

"Is that right?" She fluffed his pillow and covered him back up again.

"Yes. I'm really western born and raised."

"But I thought you came out as Mr. Westerfield's personal assistant and photographer."

"Not exactly."

"But you are the magazine photographer."

He was afraid if she knew the full story she might run him off as soon as he could ride. Also, there was a little matter of not wanting to make a liar out of Harold. "I was hired in Phoenix," he explained carefully, "to take the photographs. But we had a disagreement as I am sure you've heard."

Her smile was transformed into a look of anger. "Yes, Mr. Westerfield has told me all about that and what that . . . that man did to you with his gunbarrel. And I mean to speak to the sheriff myself about the incident. Perhaps we could file to have him arrested."

"No thanks," Clint said. "I'd rather take care of it in my own way and time."

"You had better stay clear of the Bolt riders. Old Abraham Bolt is a terror, a man as evil and vile as the devil himself. He wants this land of mine, you know."

"Why, I had the impression that he owned most of the Mogollon Rim."

"That's not true. He does own a tremendous amount of the land up here but that only seems to make him greedier for more. He would like nothing better than to own Mirror Lake and the meadows surrounding it. That, and he detests the fact that I am bringing more and more tourists every year into this country."

"But why? The town of Piney must want and need the new trade."

"Oh," Dinah said, "believe me, they do. To some of the merchants, my tourists are the difference between making a decent living and half-starving. Before I opened this resort, the only thing that Piney had going for it was the Bolt Ranch business and that of a few other cattle ranchers, loggers and prospectors. Abraham Bolt had all the power back then. Now, as I grow stronger, and more and more people come in to see how lovely this country is, Bolt's influence diminishes."

"I see. He would rather be a big fish in a small pond instead of a large one."

"Yes. Most of my guests are from Phoenix and Tucson, some from California and even farther away. They are reasonably well-heeled people, not necessarily rich, but at least very comfortable. Some of them are starting to invest in real estate up on the rim and there is a lot of it still available."

"Now I get it," Clint said, "and they're starting to drive the price of land up fast."

"Exactly. Perhaps even more important is the fact that Abraham Bolt owns a lot of land, but he leases even more from the government. His grazing rights are renegotiated every four years. The government sets the grazing fees based on the demand for land."

Clint nodded. "So, if no one else wants or needs the land, Abraham Bolt can name his price. And I'll bet his leases are about due to be renewed."

"You catch on fast," Dinah said. "Bolt wants this land to remain undiscovered and unwanted. And I'm of exactly the opposite mind."

"How did you come by this land?"

"My mother and father homesteaded it years ago. I was ten years old the first time I saw Mirror Lake and Bolt cattle were drinking from it. No one else had ever dared file for a homestead up here, especially one as valuable as this. But my father didn't know, or care about Abraham and he went ahead and filed. By the time Abraham discovered he had lost Mirror Lake and the surrounding land, it was too late. All my parents had to do was to hang on for five years and make the required homestead improvements."

Dinah took a deep breath. "We worked like animals and Abraham and his cowboys never stopped trying to chase us out. They killed our cattle and ran off our horses and milk cows. They even shot my dogs until I begged father not to get any more."

Clint studied the woman's face. He could see a lot of sadness when she remembered those childhood years. "But they made it."

"Yes," she whispered, "and Abraham never forgave them. He finally managed to have my father and mother killed. I was away at a private school in Phoenix when I received word that their buggy had slipped off an icy winter road and rolled down a mountainside. But I knew that my father would never have allowed something like that to happen. He was always especially careful when Mother was around. Their buggy was forced over the side and my parent's death was no accident. It was murder."

"But you had no proof."

She shook her head. "I'm sorry to have burdened you with my sad story. I hadn't intended to and I can honestly tell you that very few people know about it."

"Then I feel especially honored."

"I shouldn't have," she repeated, sounding angry at herself. "The golden rules of a good hostess are never to bore or burden your guests and to always act happy. I have failed on all three counts. I will be better next time."

"I hope not," Clint told her. "I'd like to become more than just another guest."

She blushed slightly and then raised an eyebrow. "You already are, Clint. You and Mr. Westerfield are going to put Dinah's Place on the map back on the eastern seaboard. After those people see your pictures and read Mr. Westerfield's glowing write up, I expect to have hundreds of new guests writing me for information and making reservations. In fact, to prepare for that, I have invested the last of my savings in new lumber and construction supplies arriving every day now. We must build at least ten more cabins before winter."

"Ten more?"

"Yes. Ones like this only larger and more elaborate."

"Very ambitious."

"I am nothing if not ambitious, Clint. I have to be. I have a five-year-old son to support and I want him to have something when I get too old to work hard anymore."

It surprised Clint that she had been married. Some women looked married and some did not. This one definitely did not. "What happened to the boy's father?"

"He died right after we were married. He was a banker and tried to prevent a robbery."

"I'm sorry."

"So are Ben and I."

Clint studied her closely. For a woman with such

vitality and good spirit, Dinah had seen a lot of tragedy in her young life.

"I'll be back soon with some breakfast," she called out as she headed for the door. "Stay in bed."

When she passed outside, the room seemed to lose its sunshine. Dinah was that radiant and Clint knew that he was going to want to spend a lot more time with her than she had to give. This was summer, the season where she had to make her year's income. Besides, she was also trying to build ten new cabins. He wondered who was going to help her do it.

Chapter Twelve

"You're not going to believe what Miss Morgan has some of the less infirm guests doing!" Harold raged, barging into Clint's cabin late that afternoon.

"Building cabins?"

Harold started at him. "How'd you know?"

"I can hear them sawing and hammering."

"Oh. Well, damnit! This is the most outrageous resort experience I have ever seen. People are doing everything out there. Hauling lumber, cooking in the kitchen, repairing furniture, rounding up cattle, milking cows, and even mending fishing boats and tackle, for God sake!"

"How is the fishing?" Clint asked hopefully.

"Who cares! Who has the time to enjoy this place? It's more like a convict work camp than a resort."

Clint grinned. "Now Harold, I imagine that anyone who does not enjoy pitching in will either leave, or be left alone. For some city people, I guess that milking a cow or fixing things is an unforgettable experience."

"Hell, they don't know what they're doing. None of them. I had to mend the boat myself or it would have sprung a leak and they'd have surely drowned."

"Then you did help."

"Sure, after I saw that I was going to be treated like a pariah if I sat on my butt in a hammock and tried to enjoy life. I don't know where she gets that type of fool out there to come here, pay her money and do the work. Wait until I write this place up. It'll sound like a forced labor camp.''

"Why don't you wait up on that," Clint suggested. "You've been here less than one day. Maybe you haven't quite seen the entire picture."

"I've seen enough. That old fool Dr. Ettinger kept trying to tell me that I needed to work hard and burn off weight. Burn it off, he said. You'd think I was a damned tallow candle or something. He kept saying that I needed more exercise.''

"Maybe he's right.''

"Well, I'm not going to stay around long enough to find out. I'm leaving right now. I'm on my way to Flagstaff and when I come back, we can go to a couple of decent resorts together. I continue to hold you to those promised interviews. You ought to be ready to travel with me by then.''

"Could be. I wish you'd stay here a little longer, though. Miss Dinah is going to be pretty upset with you leaving so soon.''

"I'll tell her that I decided to go back and get you another camera so we can take some great pictures of the lake and everything. That way, at least she'll keep treating you well. Just don't tell her what I intend to write.''

"Hey, Harold!''

Clint looked up to see a very fat man, fatter even than the magazine reporter, poking his bald spectacled head in the cabin door. "We could sure use a strong arm on raising a beam out here. Would you mind? Oh, hi there, Clint. I'm Oscar Marsh.''

Clint waved. The man was about fifty and had huge, overmagnified but very intelligent brown eyes. He looked totally benign, a fellow eminently well suited for books and an overstuffed chair. "Nice to meet you.

You look very much better."

"Thank you."

"Your face was a mess," Oscar said, his face cringing to remember the sight. "Oh, such an awful sight. Not very pretty, Clint."

The Gunsmith froze a smile. "Yeah," he said wishing the man would shut up about how bad he had looked. "It didn't feel good either."

"We hope to have your help soon," Oscar blurted. "And we are very happy to have such a strong man as Harold to help with the new cabins we will build. You two will be a great help."

"Not me, you sucker," Harold hissed under his breath before he called, "I'll be right out to help you with that beam, Oscar!"

"Nice meeting you," Oscar said with a wave of his chubby hand goodbye, then nodding so that the sunlight gleamed off his hairless pate.

"Who was that?"

"Oscar Marsh was a professor of law at Princeton. He just recently retired and moved to Phoenix not realizing how hot the summers were. Now, he's thinking of moving up here and buying some land. Land which Miss Dinah owns and comes complete with a guaranteed lifetime renewable option to the full use of Mirror Lake. Miss Dinah is selling off in five acre lots at a very nice profit. Oscar is so enthused, he's even drawing up her contracts!"

"Well, I'll be damned," Clint said. "She isn't missing a trick, is she?"

"Nope. She is obviously a very astute business woman. She should do quite nicely in the years to come. Interested in a surefire future? You might want to charm her a little, Clint."

"She'd work a man into an early grave," he decided.

"According to that idiot, Dr. Ettinger, work is what keeps a man fit and young looking."

Clint did not miss the sarcasm and chose not to take the bait. "She told me about Abraham Bolt and how he has always fought to get this land and the lake back. Has she said anything about Johnny Bolt?"

"No, and she got very quiet when I told her that you beat him in a fist fight. Quite frankly, I don't think she believed me. But several of the guests have told me that Johnny is not cut of the same cloth as his father. They say he's friendly and doesn't want this land."

"Friendly!" Clint rubbed his jaw. "That man is anything but friendly. And he was sure spoiling for trouble when he and his men caught me napping."

"I know. I thought they were going to attack me too. But it was Johnny who called off the other dogs and let me go."

"Without the mule and camera."

"Yes. I was foolish enough to tell them the reason for it and that was my mistake. They know why we are here and they have vowed to stop us."

"Is that why you are running out?" Clint asked softly.

The man's cheeks flamed. "Of course not! It is just that I've been paid to visit and write an assignment on a number of resorts. I'd risk losing my job if I stayed here all summer. Besides, I've already told you that it seems quite clear that this woman has cleverly duped a bunch of fat old fools into laboring and actually convinced them they ought to pay to do it! You should have heard that dunce Oscar Marsh telling me how he is going to be slim, tanned and healthy by this fall."

"Maybe he will be."

"Not a chance. I'll wager they will all come to their senses by the first of July and go home without paying this woman a cent. And there is one more thing."

"What's that?"

"No one is talking much about it, but I discreetly questioned the young Morgan boy and got the very distinct feeling that he is almost terrified of old Abraham Bolt. Young Ben believes that Abraham has threatened to kill his mother if she does not stop building those new cabins.''

Clint sat up straight. He felt his pulse quicken a little and he said, ''You're not just imagining this are you?''

''Heavens no! Why should I? I am merely warning you that trouble hovers very near and if the son is really nothing but a pale caricature of the old man, then I don't ever want to meet Abraham Bolt or taste his wrath. Do you?''

Clint smiled. ''Yes,'' he said, almost happily, ''I wouldn't miss it for anything.''

Harold shook his head. ''You're as daft as the rest of them. Even more so because you've been warned while they are completely ignorant of the impending danger.''

''I wish you could stay, Harold. We might need you.''

The eastern magazine writer's bloated face changed and some of the huffiness went out of his voice when he said, ''Thank you. Coming from a man as famous as yourself, Gunsmith, I shall always consider that one of the finest compliments I have ever received. It is indeed extremely flattering to think that you actually believe I might be of service to a man of action such as yourself.''

Clint shrugged. ''You can't fool me completely, Harold. You didn't get that busted nose or those scarred and broken knuckles from beating on a typewriter. You were once a man of some violence and action.''

Harold actually laughed but it came out sounding anything but happy. ''My, you are perceptive. But that was many years ago. Now, I am fat and fiftyish. A bloated bag instead of a man. Goodbye, Gunsmith. I will return here to retrieve you by the end of August. Take good care of yourself and don't let that woman con you into working off what little meat you have on your bones. And let me end by saying that, if all hell breaks loose and you need to get off of the Mogollon Rim fast, leave word of your whereabouts at the Phoenix Manor House. Also, I stand ready to return at once if you find yourself in some terrible fix. I don't know if I'd be more of a service than a disservice, but I would try.''

"I appreciate the offer," Clint said, angry with himself to think that he had privately questioned this man's bravery.

They shook hands then and Clint watched the reporter waddle out the door. It was a damned shame that he could not have been persuaded to stay and help. He and Oscar Marsh would have made quite a pair of walruses, sweating and working together, growing slim and tan and feeling better with each passing day. Dr. Ettinger was right about everyone needing some good physical activity.

But Harold Westerfield was strongly independent and very much a man despite his own cruel assessment to the contrary. And he needed freedom of choice. Besides, if Harold was right and there was gun trouble coming from old Abraham Bolt and his men, perhaps leaving was the wisest thing to do after all.

Bullshit! Clint thought. Wisdom has nothing to do with anything. It is right against wrong and that means I have to get back on my feet and be ready to work and fight, if necessary. And I sure better do it long before two weeks have passed.

Chapter Thirteen

Three days in bed with nothing to do was Clint's absolute limit. On the fourth day, he rose again before daybreak and dressed carefully. He shaved and put on clean clothes and the boots he had paid young Ben Morgan two bits to shine. Then, just as the sun was gilding the mountain peaks to the east, he stepped outside and admired the still morning lake only a hundred yards from his cabin door.

Mirror Lake was picture perfect. Almost two miles long and half that wide, it was ringed by meadow on which Dinah Morgan's cattle fattened themselves. Clint took a footpath down to the lake. He counted four big trout that jumped high out of the water and snapped for their breakfast. When he arrived at the shore, he knelt and tested the water. It was cold and clear enough to see submerged rocks twenty feet out. There was a small dock with several rowboats tied to it. Clint untied the first one he came to, then stepped into the boat and pushed it away from the dock.

The boat rocked happily and water lapped at its bow. The sunlight was growing stronger and now the bright colors of daybreak were washing across the still, glassy water. Seeing it like this, peaceful and calm, Clint knew that he was a lucky man just to be alive. He turned his attention to the boat. A wooden tackle box had all the fishing gear he needed and there was a good pole and reel in the bow. Clint found the temptation impossible to resist. He took the oars and rowed out into the lake feeling the sun warm the stiff muscles of his chest, shoulders and back.

He liked the looks of a spot nearer the opposite shore where there were cattails and a small cove and that's where he headed. Fifteen minutes later, he laid down the oars, baited his hook and cast in a long arc that demonstrated he was no stranger to fishing.

He settled back to wait. His head felt fine, no pain, no dizziness or blurring of vision. I should have done this three days ago, he thought with a contented smile.

Inside of five minutes he had a strike. A big speckled trout swallowed the bait and fought like a gaffed shark. Clint played the fish expertly and when he finally reeled it in close to the boat, it was too tired to wriggle. He caught the fish with his bare hand and unhooked it to flop around until he could cram it into an empty burlap sack which was obviously used to hold the fish. That accomplished, he cast again.

Within a half hour he had six pan-sized trout. Clint figured that he would like to catch another half dozen and that would be enough for everyone's breakfast. He could almost see how pleased that Dinah would be to have the fish for her guests.

But the next ten minutes passed without a single bite and Clint, spoiled after his early and quick success, grew impatient. Perhaps, he thought, he had fished this cove out and he needed to find another. He reeled in his hook and then rowed off to the far end of the lake and found another cove. This one was deeper, he could see the rocks perhaps ten feet below the surface and also several very large fish cruising near the bottom. It looked perfect. The cove was very secluded and ringed with tall pine trees instead of open meadow.

Clint rebaited his hook and cast. Almost before the

worm sank it was seized by a huge trout that made Clint's reel sing.

"Yahoo!" Clint called with a happy laugh. "I caught the granddaddy of 'em all!"

The fish was a whopper and he had to play it very, very carefully or it would have snapped his line. But after ten minutes, he had it beside the boat and was wishing for a net. There was none and the fish was so large he was afraid to try to swing it over the side and into the boat.

Clint leaned far out over the water, one hand holding the rod and reel skyward, the other trying to grab the slippery monster.

Finally, he managed to hook his forefinger into the trout's gills and a wide grin crossed his face. "Sorry about this," he chuckled. "But your time is up."

"So is yours, Gunsmith!"

Clint's head snapped up from the water and his eyes caught the movement of a rifle barrel poking at him. He threw himself sideways just as the rifle exploded. The bullet clipped his shoulder and Clint crashed down in the boat hearing a curse and then the ominous sound of another shell being levered. The monster trout was thrashing against the bow, trying to free itself from the hook. Clint flattened to the deck and a second bullet tore a hole right at the water line. Water rushed into the opening and the rowboat began to fill with water and sink.

Clint didn't wait for that to happen. He knew he would be riddled before the boat went under so he grabbed both gunnels and rocked violently. The boat tipped sideways and Clint was thrown into the water as more bullets began to rip the wood to splinters.

Clint swore helplessly. The water was freezing cold and he knew that the ambusher would be able to see his body through the clear water. There was nothing he could do about that except keep what remained of the boat between him and the rifleman. That, and start trying to pull himself and his shield farther out into the water.

The bullets were now coming in under the boat as the rifleman tried to hit the lower part of Clint's submerged body. But because of the angle the bullets had to travel, they lost their force in the water. When one did hit Clint, it was like being stung with a rock fired from a slingshot. It hurt, but there was no penetrating force.

Clint hung on, kicking with his feet and slowly pulling himself deeper and deeper into the lake. The monster trout was still caught and circling at the end of his line. Clint felt they both had a lot in common at the moment.

"I'll find out who you are and get you!" he shouted back to the shoreline and trees. "I promise this is not the end of it!"

"Get off the Mogollon Rim, Gunsmith. Next time, you'll be a dead man!"

Suddenly, the lake was very, very still once more. The only sound was the soft, weakening splash of the hooked granddaddy trout as it weakly circled around and around. Clint grabbed the line and pulled the fish to him. It was two foot long if it was an inch and had to weigh a good twelve pounds. He had never caught one any finer. Clint inspected its mouth. The great fish had not swallowed the worm and Clint pulled the hook free knowing the fish would live to be caught again on a better day. A day when its prize would not be overshadowed by an ambusher's bullets. The granddaddy trout seemed to find renewed life and it dove for the depths and vanished.

Clint heard a distant shout echo across the lake and when he twisted around in the water, he saw Dinah and two of her guests pile into another rowboat and come for him. Clint grabbed the tackle box, the sack of breakfast trout he had caught earlier and the good fishing pole and reel. He laid them neatly on the flat hull of his bullet-ripped boat.

This incident was going to put a major scare into the paying guests. They were old and gentle people, the kind not accustomed to gun trouble. The last thing Clint wanted was to create a panic at Dinah's Place. But there were a few things that needed to be established immediately. And the first was, who had tried to kill him and how had they already learned his true identity?

One thing sure, Clint thought, I had better find out the answers soon or my lifespan will be shorter than these fine trout we'll eat for breakfast.

Chapter Fourteen

Dinah, Dr. Ettinger and Oscar Marsh were all crowded in the boat when it reached Clint and the fact that Dinah Morgan was the only one that had thought to arm herself with a Winchester rifle did not escape Clint's attention. The way people acted in an emergency said a lot about them and while the doctor had a reason to be in the small rowboat, there was no explanation why the huge bulk of Oscar Marsh should have been invited.

"Are you all right!" Dinah yelled as the two men pulled ineffectually at the oars.

"Yes," Clint said, noting how the doctor and retired law professor were having one hell of a time keeping the rowboat moving to a straight line. "Slow down, the danger is past."

He waited for them to come up to him and then he loaded the fish and tackle into the boat. They were staring at the ruined hull he had used for protection.

Dinah bit her lip, then said. "Did you see who it was?"

"No."

"Why would anyone do this to you?" she asked.

"That's a good question." He paddled around to the stern of the boat knowing that it could not possibly hold another body without sinking. "Row over to the shore please. I'd like to have a look at the man's tracks."

Dr. Ettinger and Oscar were puffing with exertion and sweating though the air was quite cool. Clint's own teeth were chattering as they reached the shore and he slogged up and helped them beach.

"I'd like to borrow your Winchester for a minute," he said.

Dinah nodded and gave it to him. It was in good working order and well used. Clint had the feeling that Dinah was probably more than a capable shot.

"I want to come with you," she said.

"All right."

"We'll wait," Oscar gasped, mopping his brow.

"No," Dinah answered. "You and the doctor please deliver these fresh trout back to the kitchen and have them prepared for breakfast. We can walk back in short order. That is, if you are up to it, Clint."

"The activity will be good for me," Clint said.

"I'm not sure that'll be such a good idea, Clint. But what will we tell everyone?" Dr. Ettinger asked. "They are all waiting on the dock."

Dinah looked to Clint who answered, "Really, I feel fine. Why don't you just tell them that there was a deer hunter in the woods who got very reckless with his shooting."

The doctor's eyes widened. "But look at that hull you were clinging too! No one. . . ."

Suddenly, his mouth clamped shut. "Yes," he whispered, "I understand. There is no sense in creating a panic among the guests."

"Right. If someone wants to kill me or even just drive me off the rim, it has nothing to do with anyone else. Isn't that right, Miss Morgan?"

She nodded quietly and he could see the struggle which now raged within her. Clint had a hunch Dinah knew who could answer some of his questions and he needed to talk to her alone.

When they got the boat turned and the two rowers headed for open water, Clint started into the woods. He walked in silence, listening to the forest sounds, sure that there was no further danger but too well-schooled by his years as a lawman not to play things safe.

"Here's where he fired from," Clint said, kneeling down and picking up a spent cartridge and finding nothing about it that was unusual.

Dinah studied his face. "Is it true what you said about not seeing the rifleman?"

"Yes, I'm afraid so. The man was in the deep shadows of this forest and I was in bright sunlight. It was impossible to see anything. Do you know who it was, Dinah?"

She blinked. "Why should I?"

"Because Harold Westerfield told me something more about your past. I know that your son is frightened by Abraham Bolt and that you have been threatened."

She swallowed noisily, then her chin lifted. "That is all true, but I fail to see how it involves you unless. . . ."

"Unless what?"

"Unless you are not who you say you are."

Clint took her arm and they followed the trail of the ambusher a few hundred yards before Clint knelt beside an especially clear hoofprint. He studied it a long time. "The horse he rode cups its hooves outward and is long overdue for new shoes. See how this one is cracked? And his left shoe has a nail missing."

She knelt down beside him and studied the hoofprint carefully. "Yes, I can see that. What are you doing now?"

Clint took a single pine needle and laid it across the track. He broke it off exactly at the outside edges of the shoemark and slipped it into his soggy shirt pocket. "A horse's hoofprints are about as individual as a man's fingerprints. Trouble is, he has four of them and whenever a man changes the shoes on his horse, the print changes with it. But when you get a really worn shoe like this horse was wearing, it is pretty distinctive.''

She nodded. "I understand, but what are you going to do, go into Piney and walk around examining horses' feet?''

"No, but if I happen across this same horse's track and it is still fresh, I'll recognize it immediately.''

Dinah stood up. She was all woman but surprisingly petite for a young woman who shouldered so much responsibility. "You are not really a photographer, are you?''

"Nope.''

"You are a lawman.'' It was not a question.

"I was,'' he admitted.

"Is that the reason this ambusher chose you?''

"I honestly don't know.'' Clint took her arm and they started back toward the lake. It would be a fairly long walk and he wanted to get back before all his trout were devoured. "That's the most obvious possibility. About as real as the possibility that whoever did this cares less about my past and more about my future here.''

She thought for several minutes as they walked along the shoreline. "Do you think that the ambusher might have been trying to run you off rather than gain revenge for something out of your past?''

"He warned me to get off the Mogollan Rim or I'd be shot,'' Clint said. "Now he might have been trying to sidetrack me and throw suspicion to the Bolts, but I have to assume it was Johnny Bolt and act accordingly.''

He stopped very suddenly. "It wasn't Johnny,'' she said in a very certain voice. "I know that much. He is not an ambusher. He is hotheaded and irresponsible. He can be. . . . why are you looking at me like that, Clint?''

"I was wondering how you came to know him so

well. Especially since the Bolts have always been your family's enemy and finally did succeed in killing your mother and father.''

Her lips tightened with anger. "What else did Mr. Westerfield tell you!"

"That you intend to sell Oscar Marsh and future guests five acre lots with access to the lake at a nice profit."

"That's no secret! And they are going to get every penny of value."

Clint shrugged. "Of course they are. But I sort of thought it might be the reason why Abraham Bolt is so determined to run you out."

"That's a part of it."

"And the other part?"

She started walking. "With all due respect, the other part is none of your business, Clint."

He grabbed her by the elbow and turned her around. "Yes, it is. I could have been shot an hour ago and the next time I may not be so lucky. I need to hear the other reasons why Abraham wants you ruined."

"He wants Mirror Lake and my surrounding meadow land. It's just that simple!" She looked very angry. "And now, let me ask you a question. Who are you, really, and when are you leaving?"

Clint released her. "My name is Clint Adams. I am better known as the Gunsmith."

She blinked. "You're the Gunsmith?"

"Yes."

"That explains it then! You'd have dozens of mortal enemies. One of them must have recognized you in Piney and sent the word out that you were here. All you have to do is to leave and things will be fine again."

"Do you really believe that?"

"Well, of course! I have never had anyone threaten one of my guests before this morning. So after you're gone, we can get back to normal around here."

"I don't think so, Dinah. I think that the day that Oscar Marsh rides into Piney to record the deed to the property you sell him, he is as good as dead."

Dinah paled. "If I believed that even for one minute, I would never sell the land to him."

"Are you prepared to gamble with Oscar's life? Can't you just keep the land awhile longer and make enough money on the guests?"

She started walking and he fell in beside her. Dinah had a fine walk, her strides long and purposeful. "I could next year with the additional cabins," she admitted. "In fact, to be honest, I have been sort of concerned about Oscar buying that land. And since your arrival, I've become deeply worried. I wish he would forget about it."

"Tell him you've changed your mind."

"I can't. When we first discussed this, he was so excited that he drew up a legal document—he's a distinguished law professor, you know."

"I know."

"Anyway," she continued, "he drew it up and gave me a hundred dollars for a three year option to buy. It's legal, and while he is a dear, dear man, he is also the kind who would enforce the option just on the basis of principle."

"Even if you warned him he might be killed?"

Dinah nodded. "I know this is difficult to understand because he is so well-meaning but ineffectual. But the truth of it is that when it comes to the law, Mr. Marsh has this blind faith that everyone operates according to the rules. I am sure he has heard of murderers, seen and read about criminals, but he was a university professor and that was all theoretical. He was insulated from reality so long that he can't seem to conceive that a man like Abraham Bolt is evil and will kill if necessary to achieve his aims. Oscar Marsh would not believe that anyone would kill another person over a five acre piece of forest.''

''And he'd discover he was wrong at the moment of his death,'' Clint said, shaking his head in amazement.

''Something like that, yes.''

They walked on a while in silence. Clint realized that Dinah still had not explained how she knew Johnny Bolt so very well. Also, Clint was sure that the attack had been to either kill or run him off so that he did not side with Dinah Morgan against the Bolt interests.

Clint did not appreciate being ambushed. He was probably going to catch a chill and unless the sun warmed him up a little faster, possibly even pneumonia.

But most troubling of all was the inescapable fact that Dinah seemed to believe that if he just left the Mogollon Rim this problem would resolve itself.

She was wrong. Clint glanced sideways at her. Somehow, he had to make Dinah Morgan understand that she must get help or risk leaving behind a five-year-old orphan.

Chapter Fifteen

The fish were delicious, but it seemed as if Clint was the only one that noticed. He had explained about the possibility of an errant deer hunter and the guests had accepted that as the most likely reason for the gunfire. It was fortunate, Clint thought, that they had not seen the riddled rowboat. But even though no one save the four of them realized that the shooting had been of murderous intent, the guests were clearly upset.

"If that could happen once," a retired yacht builder from San Diego said, "it could happen again and to any one of us. And some of us cannot even swim anymore!"

Clint tried to help Dinah calm them but it wasn't easy. It was not until breakfast was over and they all got to work outside that the worries subsided. Clint saw at once how the cabins were being constructed. Dinah had hired men from Piney to bring in the lumber and erect the framework. The cabins would each include two separate rooms and a fireplace. The fireplaces had already been constructed by rockmasons from Phoenix. All in all, it was clear that this was a very expensive undertaking.

He set right to work with the others carrying siding and nailing it up. The roofs were going to be harder for few of the volunteers were strong or agile enough to climb ladders. Clint found the morning passed quickly.

He soon learned that the guests worked very slowly; they argued in a good-natured fashion over the smallest construction details and spent about as much time talking as working. They took rest periods often and many vanished for hours at a time to nap.

But there were about forty guests and even with half of them idle at any one time, the work was going very fast, many of the women working side by side with the men. Clint had not been a man who built many things, but he found he enjoyed the labor although he could not hammer without his head beginning to pound and his ears ring.

"You are making a big mistake getting out of bed and back to work so soon, young man!" Dr. Ettinger said sharply. "You might give yourself a relapse."

"I'm sorry. I just can't stay down."

"No one ever listens to a doctor. No one!" Ettinger shuffled away mumbling to himself.

That night and every night for the next two weeks Clint fell into an exhausted sleep and dreamed of catching the granddaddy trout all over again and afterward, of making love to Dinah Morgan.

His headaches diminished, then disappeared completely. Despite the hard work, he found himself gaining his weight back and he knew it was muscle being added instead of fat. Dinah was everywhere, a whirlwind of perpetual motion, always laughing and urging the workers on. Even so, Clint could not figure out how she got them to do this until one day a guest casually revealed that Dinah was issuing stock and that each day's work earned stock credits.

"Of course," the man said with a happy shrug of his shoulders, "if she doesn't make a success of it then all this is wasted effort. But then, she runs the risk of losing money while all we lose is a little honest sweat."

"So that's it," Clint said.

"Sure, it is! All of us could afford to go somewhere

and never lift a finger. We could sit around and be waited upon hand and foot but we wouldn't get this sense of accomplishment that we have here at Dinah's Place. Why, we'll be charter members. That means we will always have the option of buying a five acre parcel in paradise. Not only that, but we'll have all the club privileges and also get our names engraved in a marble monument that'll stand right out in front of the clubhouse and lodge.''

"Clubhouse and lodge?'' No one had mentioned either one to Clint until now.

"Sure! This year the cabins, next year the clubhouse and lodge, the year after that . . .''

"Whoa up there!'' Clint said with a laugh. "I get the picture. Dinah has a whole lot of big plans.''

"You bet she does! She'll be a rich woman some day and some of us old codgers think of her almost as a daughter.''

Clint wondered if that meant that Dinah was going to be included in their wills and reap a sizable inheritance. He bet she would.

"Don't you folks ever leave this place for a little excitement?'' He had watched them sing around the campfires and play pinocle, dominos and poker but that got old after awhile.

"This next week we are all taking a hayride into Piney and eating at the cafe. Can't go in much on the weekends, though.''

"Why not?''

"It isn't safe. Bolt men are there on Saturday nights along with some of the other ranching crews. On Sunday morning, old Abraham Bolt brings his family in for church services. Then, I hear the women all get sent back in wagons and the men get roaring drunk and tear up the town. They have it all put back together by Wednesday, though, and that's when we are going to visit. Maybe you'd like to come along too.''

Clint nodded. His mind was turning over this new information very carefully. Damned if he did not want to see Abraham and have a little talk with the rancher. Clint was very certain that Abraham was the one who stood behind all the trouble so far. It was Clint's opinion that the best way to solve differences with another man was to meet him face to face and try to settle things with words. Usually, it could be done peaceably but if not, it was still better to face the man and be done with the issue. Maybe on a Sunday, old Abraham would abide by the word of God not to kill. It seemed like a good time to find out.

"Does Abraham bring any of his men in with him on Sunday?"

"Sure. He always does. Why are you asking?"

"Just curious is all." Clint grabbed a board and went back to work. He figured there was no sense in telling anyone about his plans. Dinah and her boy would get all upset and worried.

When Clint thought about little Ben Morgan, he felt good inside. Right away they had struck a great friendship. Maybe it was because Clint was about the same age as the boy's father would have been if he had lived. Maybe too it was because Clint whittled the boy a wooden gun to play with the first evening he had the headache go away. Dinah hadn't especially liked the gift, but that was not surprising since her husband had died by a bank robber's gun. The woman did not forbid her son playing with the gun, however, but you could tell she wasn't especially happy about it.

"This Mogollon Rim is a rough and lawless country," Clint had explained. "If you want everything all nice and safe, you should never have returned here and taken on the Bolt family."

"This land was won by my mother and father. They fought for it, died for it. I couldn't live with myself if I had turned away."

"You did the right thing. But don't blame guns for the trouble. Blame the Bolts and people like them. The only thing that kind respects is force. Young Ben there is going to have to grow up big and strong enough to shoulder the responsibility of keeping up what you have built for him. And sometimes, a man has to be willing to fight and die for that."

Clint remembered her response. "If he fights and is killed, what has he won except an early grave?"

"You know the answer to that, Dinah. So did your parents. They left something and they lived honorably, with their heads even if their backs were to the wall."

She had looked ashamed. "Yes. I know what you say is true. But sometimes . . . sometimes I get very tired of the bloodshed. I have lost three of the dearest people I'll ever love, Ben is all I have left. I would rather give up all this than lose him. Is that wrong?"

"No," Clint had told her, feeling chastised. "Of course not."

That night Clint had oiled his gun and buckled his gunbelt around his hip. He had stood facing the log wall of his cabin and practiced his draw a few times. He would have liked to have gone outside and practiced his marksmanship as well, but that would have alarmed everyone and given his intentions away.

Maybe he would find Abraham reasonable and they could settle their differences peaceably, but Clint doubted it. Then too, there was the matter of Arnie and the pistol-whipping Clint had received from the man. If Arnie came to town Sunday, Clint was going to return some pain in full measure.

Nope, any way you figured it, the Gunsmith thought, come Sunday all hell is going to break loose in Piney.

Chapter Sixteen

Clint had not said a word to anyone about his intention to ride into Piney because he wanted no one to worry—or interfere. He had seen very good men die because of some well intentioned but tragic interference by a friend, wife or a lover. So after breakfast on Sunday, when most of the guests were still lingering over their coffee and talking about fishing or getting up a hot game of horseshoes, Clint quietly slipped out and hurried to the stables.

Dinah kept about ten good saddlehorses for her guests to use. They were mostly old cow ponies who had broken down in the joints and couldn't do much more than trot. Clint moved through the stables and found Duke in a box stall eating his breakfast. Seeing him, Duke nickered hopefully.

"What's the matter," Clint said, bridling the horse and leading it out to be saddled. "Life a little too slow here? No friends your own age to converse with?"

The gelding bobbed its magnificent head and Clint smiled. He led the horse over to a tie ring and began to curry it, starting with the mane and tail, then back to the neck and down across the body. The horse stomped its feet with anticipation and when Clint hauled out his blankets and saddle, Duke knew that they were finally going for an outing. "It'll be a short one today," he said, cinching up tight and noticing that Duke had added a couple of inches around his girth.

"Then why didn't you invite me and Ben along?"

Clint swiveled around on his bootheel to see Dinah and the boy watching him. Damn! he thought, trying to think of a good answer. "Well, sometimes a man needs to get off by himself, Dinah."

"That is not very flattering. You could have gone for a walk in the woods. Or at least told us you were going."

He sharpened his tone of voice. "You're not my keeper. I go where and when I want and I don't ask anyone's permission."

Clint could see how his words struck her hard but he did not regret them if they got him away without a full explanation.

"Excuse me for caring about you!" Dinah said, hurt and angry. "But you have already been shot at once and if anything should happen . . ."

He smiled, not wishing to part with this fine woman on a bad note and fully aware that a lot could happen to him in Piney—most of it possibly fatal.

Clint led Duke over and brushed her cheek with his forefinger, the one he used to pull the trigger of his six-gun. "I'm sorry, Dinah. I just need to be off by myself awhile and this being Sunday, it seemed like a good time."

"You wouldn't go to Piney, would you?" Her eyes were wide with a mix of dread and suspicion. "Clint, Abraham Bolt and his men will be there today and you know that would be trouble."

Clint knelt beside Ben. The boy had the same features of his mother, but he was going to be tall, well over six feet with light brown hair and dark blue eyes. He was a good looking kid even if a little too serious. "I'll bring you back some rock candy," he promised.

Dinah's voice sounded flat and defeated when she said, "Then you are going to Piney."

He stood up, running his hands through Ben's hair. "Yeah."

"Why?"

"Because this is a free country and I won't be kept out of anywhere. And because I always like to face trouble squared up rather than be shot at from ambush."

"They might kill you."

"They might try," he corrected.

"No one is fast or good enough with a gun to take on Bolt and his entire bunch of hardcases."

She squeezed his hand between her own. "As a favor to me and Ben. Don't go."

He kissed her on the lips. It wasn't something he had planned on doing, nor was it a passionate kiss. But just happened and it seemed right. Before she could say another word he climbed on Duke and rode out of the barn without looking back.

It was a fine day, big lumbering clouds overhead gave promise of afternoon showers. The lake was still, its tranquility broken only when one of those big trout broke water and grabbed an insect, then whopped down noisily. Clint felt loose and relaxed. He also felt like he was doing the right thing.

He was a man who liked to resolve issues and live a very uncomplicated life. Back at the resort, Dinah was worried, but Clint wasn't. A man died as he lived, fast or slow. I'll take fast any old day, Clint thought as he swung onto the road leading to Piney.

When he reached the outskirts of town, he reined Duke in and studied the layout. It was a common enough looking town. One main street with a post office, two or three saloons and general stores. The streets were empty because the cowboys, prospectors and everyone else slept late on Sunday after hell-raising the night before.

But at the far end of town, a church bell began to toll and now as Clint watched, he saw quite a few people exiting from the houses and stores. They were going to a small white church with a fine steeple and cross. The church was right at the end of town by a little cemetery at the edge of the pines.

A wagon or two came in from out to the east, but then Clint saw a carriage pulled by two matched palominos emerge from the northern forest. Inside the carriage were two men and three ladies and outside, a dozen riders rode slightly behind in the dust. The carriage sparkled, its brasswork was well polished and the team of palomino's shone like beaten gold from a hard morning's brushing.

"That's them," Clint said to Duke as he watched the carriage draw up to the church. "And they're going to praise the Lord. Sure hope they are in a Christian frame of mind when they come back outside again."

He noted how the congregation filed slowly past the minister who dutifully shook everyone's hand as they entered. Clint would have liked to have gone to that church just to hear a rousing, fire-and-brimstone sermon. It did a man's soul good to hear the Word now and then.

But Clint decided that he had better stay outside of the church this morning. There were many women and children in attendance and if old Abraham was as wild and short-fused as his son, then the rancher might even open fire, or curse and embarrass the congregation. No, Clint thought, I will meet him among men, and then we will see what happens. Clint saw the door to the church close. He nudged Duke with his bootheels and rose on into Piney. The saloons were open but not much else. Clint did not drink in the morning so he rode around behind the church and tied Duke.

The congregation had begun to sing in full voice, "Rock of Ages," a fine song. Clint stretched out on the grass and closed his eyes. Maybe he could still get a little religion just by being close to the pulpit.

Chapter Seventeen

They ended the service with a hymn called "Lord, Pass Me Some Cornbread." Clint had never heard the gospel song, and he figured it was all right if he never did again.

He stood up and brushed off the grass and squared his hat, then mounted Duke and rode a wide loop back into town. He tied his horse on a side street because it was his belief that a man outgunned had better not get caught by his enemies during the awkward seconds it took to remount.

There were two saloons and he chose the Elk Horn because it was closer. At the bar, he ordered a cup of coffee from a taciturn bartender before sauntering to the rearmost table where the light was very dim. He hoped that Abraham Bolt preferred this saloon to the other, it would make things simpler. Clint noted that the room had a back door with a sign that informed its customers there was a privy for their convenience in the alley.

Clint sipped his coffee slowly. He guessed he ought to have some kind of speech or something rehearsed for Abraham Bolt, but he could think of none. Really, all that needed to be said was that he wanted to return a favor to Arnie for pistol-whipping him from behind that first day in the meadow. And if Johnny wanted to finish

their fight later on, that was all right too. The last thing
that needed saying was going to be a little trickier. What
Clint wanted to let the tyranical old rancher know was
that he was going to be hanging around Dinah's Place
for the summer working on those cabins. There had
damn sure better be no more ambushes.

Clint chose the right saloon. Fifteen minutes after he
came to roost, heavy steps sounded on the boardwalk
and then the batwing doors banged open. Just for an instant, Abraham Bolt was framed in the doorway and the
man was so huge he blocked out the mid-morning sun.
He had gone to fat though, and when he pushed inside,
Clint saw that his face was bloated and wasted by too
much drinking and maybe too many hours in the sun.

"Set 'em up on me!" he thundered. "Goddamn if the
Reverend Gompers didn't give a tail-twister of a sermon
today!"

Abraham waited impatiently for the glasses to be
filled. He lost his patience, seized the bottle roughly and
poured. His method was to set the glasses side by side
and slash whiskey over them as though they were garden
flowers.

"Sinners," he bellowed. "Today, let us drown the
devil in ourselves and howl hallelujah brothers!"

Clint watched the rancher and his men upend the
glasses and then before they could wipe their faces with
their sleeves, the bartender was splashing another
round. Clint did not see Johnny, but he figured the
younger Bolt was somewhere about. He did manage to
recognize the one called Arnie and the other men who
had caught him napping that afternoon.

Clint debated how long to let the men drink before he
made his own presence known. It was clear that they
would not pay him any mind for they were intent on
their drinking and banter. With some men, you were best
let them drink awhile because it gave you the edge if

they tried to go to their guns. Drunk men not only shot poorly, they often dropped their weapons or discharged them into their own feet. Other men, however, got more dangerous and it was best to reason with them when they were cold sober. Clint sort of had the feeling that Abraham Bolt was going to get very drunk and very mean as the day wore on. But there was something else to consider and that was how to get the man's undivided attention.

Clint stood up and pushed back his chair thinking, what the hell, no one lives forever. He drew his gun and when Arnie raised his glass, Clint's well placed bullet shattered it. For an instant, Arnie just stared with disbelief at the stub of broken glass in his fist and then he lurched around to see the Gunsmith.

"Everyone freeze!" Clint ordered, his sixgun beginning to move cobra-like in his hand.

Surprisingly, they all took his advice except for one would-be gunman who tried to draw and fire. Clint's bullet shattered the man's fist and sent him staggering out the door, screaming for the town doctor.

"Who the hell are you!" Abraham bellowed, his hand shifting toward the gun he wore.

"Clint Adams. The Gunsmith. Take your choice. The only thing that matters is that I and Miss Dinah Morgan are left in peace."

"What the hell has that got to do with shooting a man's whiskey glass out of his hand!"

"Arnie and I have a score to settle," Clint said quietly. "Don't we."

The man nodded and fear spurred the ropy muscles of his hawk-face. "I won't draw on you, Gunsmith."

Clint holstered his gun. Although he was furious with Arnie for the way he had viciously pistol-whipped him he was not nearly stupid enough to just wade in swinging his fists. He could probably whip Arnie, but after doing so, Abraham would have the complete advantage.

"Draw," Clint said, "or die with your gun holstered."

Arnie threw his hands up over his head. "No! I wouldn't stand a chance! Mr. Bolt, do something!"

Clint forgot about Arnie for the moment. "Your man likes to break heads, Mr. Bolt. I've been forced to pistol-whip a lot of rowdy cowboys in my time but I never tried to brain-damage any of them the way Arnie did to me. Are you buying into this or not?"

There wasn't a man in the saloon who didn't understand that, if the shooting started, Abraham Bolt would be the first one to die. The Gunsmith was simply unbeatable even though he would be throwing his own life away after his third or fourth bullet. And the question also was, after Abraham and Arnie, who else would the Gunsmith kill? That was the question on every Bolt cowboy's mind.

"Tell you what," Abraham said, "I'll have someone go find the sheriff and arrest this man."

"Boss!"

"Shut up!" Abraham thundered. "Did you do what he said or not?"

"Sure," Arnie said, "I hit him but. . . ."

Abraham took a deep breath, then he grabbed the whiskey bottle and with surprising quickness for a man of his age, brought it down on Arnie's head with a powerful blow that shattered glass and liquor across the floor. Arnie dropped as if pole-axed.

"That is the last favor I'll ever do for you, Gunsmith, except to tell you to be off the Mogollon Rim by tomorrow night."

"And if I'm not?"

"Then you've been warned. I mean to have the Morgan woman's land. I've offered her a fair price. I've been patient and reasonable because I'm a gentleman with real ladies and she is that. But my patience is worn out. Tell her so."

"She won't sell or be run off any more than I will," Clint said. "She means to have the finest resort in Arizona and I intend to see she does."

Abraham Bolt poured two glasses of whiskey and offered one to Clint. His voice shook but was under control when he said, "I like a man who lays his cards down on the table, Gunsmith. Johnny told me you wouldn't do things the easy way but I didn't believe him. What will convince you to be smart instead of dead?"

Clint reached for the glass with his left hand and when the old pirate made his play, Clint was ready. His own hand flashed for his sixgun and he jammed the barrel into Abraham's distended belly almost to its cylinder. The gun cocked and Abraham paled and froze.

"You're a deceitful and treacherous old bastard," Clint whispered. "And I wouldn't trust you farther than I could throw you. Next time you or any of your men try to use a gun on me, someone is going to die. Understand?"

Abraham nodded. He understood all right. But something red and wild in his eyes told Clint that he didn't give a good goddamn.

Clint backed toward the door and pushed it open, his gun still on Abraham. When the doors swung shut, he started to turn and move fast but that's when he heard a shout.

There were quite a few townspeople on the street, many of them having just left the church services. But Clint barely noticed them as his attention instantly fixed on Johnny Bolt and another man who looked like a gunslick. The gunslick went for his sidearm and Clint had no choice but to put a bullet into him. The man staggered, dead where he had stood. Johnny Bolt caught him as he fell and then made the mistake of going for his own gun.

"Don't!" Clint yelled in warning. A woman screamed and grabbed her child. Men in their Sunday suits dove for the ground.

Johnny Bolt was already committed to making his play. He was fast too, but had no chance at all. Clint used an extra split second and aimed high and for the shoulder. He saw blood blossom on Johnny's coat and his bullet sent the rancher's son corkscrewing full around and then crashing over a water trough.

The Elk Horn exploded with gunfire. Clint knew that nothing on this earth could stop old Abraham Bolt for having his vengeance now. Clint sized up the impossible odds and ducked into a side alley. He heard shouting and the pounding boots of a dozen running men. It was time to move along. Trouble was, he did not dare to go back to Dinah's Place or he would just be dragging trouble like a dog with a can tied to its tail.

No, Clint thought, I had best lay low for a couple of days until the storm passes.

Chapter Eighteen

He circled the town and headed out in the opposite direction of Dinah's Place, but only after he was sure that they were hot on his trail. Clint followed the road letting Duke flatten his ears and run like the wind. With every stride the big gelding carried him farther ahead of his pursuers. When he had a half mile lead, he came upon a stream and followed it into the trees. The Bolt riders galloped on past and Clint doubled back toward Piney, riding slow and easy.

Clint tied his horse at the far end of town and headed for the sheriff's office. So far, he had not seen a trace of the man and it was time that they had a private talk before things got any more exciting.

Because no one expected him to return and he kept his hat pulled low over his eyes, he was not noticed. He barged into the sheriff's office and caught the man off guard. Clint closed the door softly behind him. "Howdy," he said. "Got a couple of minutes to palaver?"

The sheriff was scribbling some kind of paperwork and when he looked up, he was so surprised to see Clint that the pencil fell from his hand. "You," he whispered. "Are you crazy! Every man on the Bolt payroll is looking for you right now!"

"You aren't," Clint answered grimly.

The sheriff flushed with shame and embarrassment. "I ought to arrest you," he said lamely.

"For what? Killing one man and wounding another in self defense? Sheriff, there are at least a dozen witnesses who saw the entire thing out on the street. Now, I realize that this is Bolt's town, but he must have a lot of enemies. People who are sick and tired of having him run rough-shod over Piney like it was his personal kingdom."

"I'm the law here, not Abraham."

"Cut the crap, Sheriff. Bolt owns you and everyone knows it."

The man's face stiffened. He was in his forties, lean and nervous-looking with the complexion of a man with a sour stomach. His office was a pig sty and there was dried food all over the front of his coat and shirt. Hell, even his badge was tarnished and dull looking.

"Why don't you turn yourself in?" he said, showing tobacco-stained teeth. "All Abraham really wants is for you to leave the Mogollon Rim. I'll see you get off this mountain alive."

"And then what happens to Dinah Morgan? You gonna let Abraham run her the hell out—or kill her if she still keeps refusing to cooperate?"

"Abraham won't hurt her," the sheriff said quickly. "Johnny would never let that happen."

Clint blinked with surprise. "Why?"

"Never mind that. Let's just say that they were once pretty close friends."

"That's not what I heard." Clint rubbed his jaw. "It's my understanding that their families have always been enemies."

"Yeah, but not Dinah and Johnny. Kids don't always learn to hate the way their folks do. I think . . ." The man clamped his mouth shut."

"What do you think?"

"Nothing."

Clint stepped forward and his face was threatening. "Come on, tell me if it's important."

"All right, but it's nothing more than an educated opinion. You were a lawman for years, you know how you get to noticing things that other people miss. It's a sense about people that every lawman develops."

"Get to the point."

"It's just that I think Johnny and Dinah might have had a thing going between them when they were younger. And I'm not too convinced that it ever ended."

Clint's eyes narrowed. "She married another man."

"Maybe she wanted to hurt Johnny and knew that was the worst way she could do it."

Clint twisted around and strode to the window considering the possibility as the sheriff's voice chased after him. "Listen, Gunsmith," he said, "I have nothing but the greatest respect for Dinah Morgan. They don't come any better than her. If that fine woman looked at me twice, I'd fall all over myself trying to impress her. All I'm telling you is that Johnny is keeping her alive and, if it wasn't for him, old Abraham would have run her off a long, long time ago."

"And you wouldn't have done a damn thing to stop him."

"Wouldn't and couldn't. I'm no fool. I try to keep this town peaceable and I'm not a coward that hides when trouble comes into Piney. But I'll not be a martyr either. I don't want to die."

"Nobody does," Clint said in a tight voice. "But if you ask me, I think you're a disgrace to the law profession."

The sheriff began to inspect his fingernails. "You can think what you want. I'm telling you as honest as I can how the land lies up here on the Mogollon Rim. This is Bolt country and you have made yourself his enemy. Abraham will never forgive you for shooting Johnny."

"How is he?"

"In a lot of pain. But your bullet just cut through shoulder muscle. Didn't even hit the bone. Lucky thing for him or he'd have been crippled for life."

"Luck had nothing to do with it."

"I believe you," the sheriff said with a nod of understanding. "But Abraham never will. He'll nail your hide to a barn door."

Clint expelled a deep breath. "I'm in a tight corner," he admitted wearily. "I can't go straight back to Dinah's Place because that's the first spot they'll come looking. And yet, I don't dare leave or Abraham will destroy Dinah. Got any ideas?"

"Yeah, turn yourself in to me and I'll get a federal judge up here right away. They'll be a trial and if it happened like you say, you'll be set free. After that, Abraham won't dare touch you."

Clint studied the man. Could the sheriff be trusted? What if he did surrender and the man shot him? It had happened plenty of times and probably would again.

"I'll think about it," he said, heading for the door.

"It's the only way, Gunsmith. Where are you going now?"

"I want to pay a visit to Johnny Bolt. Where did they take him?"

"Over to the hotel. They put him in Room Two, there are only six rooms in the whole place. You won't have any trouble finding him."

"Thanks."

Five minutes later, Clint was pushing inside the hotel room to find Johnny lying with his eyes shut and a big bandage on his shoulder. No one would ever have expected Clint to show up in Piney again, not alive, that is. And so when Clint cleared his throat, Johnny didn't even open his eyes.

"How are you feeling?" Clint asked.

Johnny's eyes snapped open. He twisted his head around and disbelief flashed across his features. With a cry of surprise, he lunged for the sixgun hanging on his bedpost. Clint anticipated this and snatched the gun away first. "Whoa up now, I come in peace," he said.

"Peace! You're a dead man, Gunsmith!"

Clint shrugged. "The sheriff sorta told me the same thing. I didn't believe him either. I've also been told that you are a better man than your father. I thought maybe we could work something out between us."

Johnny Bolt stared at him, not sure he had heard correctly. "You shoot me, kill one of our men and now you want to be friends? You must be loco!"

"Nope. I killed your man in self defense. You saw that. I could have killed you next, but I didn't even choose to shatter your shoulder. So far, I've done about everything that I can possibly think of to avoid bloodshed."

"I don't believe I'm hearing this," Johnny said, "you are my enemy and. . . ."

"I'm not your enemy! All I'm trying to do is to keep Dinah Morgan and her son Ben alive. They own Mirror Lake and they've chosen to make a resort out of it. You can't stop progress. I had hoped you might be able to talk some sense into your father."

"He never listens to anyone, least of all me. Besides, why should I even try?"

"Because you never got over loving Dinah Morgan."

When Clint said it, he was not sure what kind of reaction he would get, but he knew there would be a strong one. He was wrong. Johnny just went stiff and his face became even paler.

"Who told you?" Johnny asked quietly.

So, Clint thought, the sheriff's suspicions were correct. "Does it matter?"

Johnny looked away, his handsome face wore a stricken look, one that said better than words how much he loved Dinah Morgan. "No, it doesn't," he said in a solemn voice.

"Is she the reason you never married?"

"Maybe."

"Did you have anything to do with killing her husband or parents?"

Johnny swung his head around and glared at Clint. "Hell no! I hated Robert Morgan. He was an arrogant, overeducated little bastard and I never could see why she married him. Sure he had a lot of money and influence down in Phoenix. They said he was going to be a United States Senator some day—governor before he was fifty years old! But he was a snobbish little runt and when I went to the wedding, I told him so."

"You voiced those words at the man's wedding?"

"Damn right I did! He wouldn't fight me, though. He just sneered and said I was nothing but uneducated, unwashed trash. Hell, he didn't even know that me and Dinah had gone off to college together the year before."

"Where?"

"Boston. Dinah went first—to Boston College and I followed later—to Harvard. But my father found out why I left and threatened to . . ." Johnny stopped in midsentence, aware that he had trapped himself.

"Threatened to what?" Clint demanded.

"Nothing."

"To disinherit you?"

"No, goddammit! To kill Dinah's folks."

There was a long silence between them before Clint whispered, "I'm sorry. I should have guessed. So you left her and came back to the ranch. And you never told Dinah why."

"How could I tell her the real reason? Next thing I know, she's engaged to be married to Robert Morgan. There wasn't a thing to be done for it. Then after her parents died in that accident . . ."

"She says that they were murdered."

Johnny looked away. "I don't know about that," he said. "It couldn't have been proved either way. A man gives his father the benefit of the doubt in something like that.''

Clint walked over to the window and stared out into the street. "You are a good man, Johnny. And I'm sorry that it worked out between you and Dinah like it did. It's a real tragedy. It has always been my opinion that our first, innocent loves are often our best loves. And yet we usually lose them, never realizing the mistake until later."

"Get out of this country," Johnny said miserably. "There is nothing you can do to stop what is going to happen."

Clint spun around, his anger unleashed. "I won't leave. And if you don't help Dinah, she *will* eventually push your father's patience to the breaking point and he'll order her to be killed. Her death will be made to appear like another accident just like that of her mother and father. Do you want to live with that on your conscience for the rest of your life?"

Johnny said nothing. But his despair was clear.

"Think about it real hard," Clint said. "We'll be talking again before long."

He closed the door behind him and walked through the lobby no longer caring who recognized him. Clint had made the big decision—he was going to take his chances and turn himself in to the sheriff for trial.

But first, he was going to make sure that nothing bad happened at Dinah's Place.

Chapter Nineteen

Dinah Morgan tried to go about the job of entertaining her guests on Sunday afternoon but her mind was not on the task. She was worried sick about Clint's visit to Piney. Every few minutes her eyes would turn toward the town hoping to see the Gunsmith galloping, Duke up the road.

"Ben wants to go fishing with some of us," one of her guests said, "do you mind? I swear that boy knows every good fishing spot on the entire lake."

She was sitting on the porch of her log cabin with Oscar Marsh. "No, by all means, take Ben. If you catch enough, perhaps we can cook them over an outdoor fire this evening."

The guest, a prominent merchant from Tucson named Frank Hammer, smiled. "I didn't think you'd mind. Ben said he had some chores left to do but I said that if he helped me catch a mess of fish, I'd help him with his chores."

"That sounds like a good arrangement for both of you," Dinah said, still watching the road into town.

When Hammer and several of her guests had gone off in two rowboats, another pair of guests stopped by to ask Dinah if she would like to play a game of cribbage, but she declined.

Oscar Marsh set down a book he had been reading

and which was titled *Ragged Dick*, by Horatio Alger. "You're very worried about our friend, Clint Adams, aren't you?"

"Is it that obvious?"

The ex-law professor removed his .thick reading glasses. "Oh yes, quite. May I ask why?"

"I'm afraid there may be danger in town for Clint with Abraham Bolt and his crew of troublemakers. Very serious trouble."

"There is a sheriff to make sure that such things are settled lawfully, isn't there?"

Dinah smiled at the man's innocence, "Yes, but out west the law sometimes looks away from trouble."

"You mean Clint might actually be in physical jeopardy?"

"Exactly."

"Oh, my," Oscar said in a worried voice, "now I understand your agitation. Is there anything I can do? Would it make you feel easier if I tried to saddle one of your horses and ride into town? Perhaps I could prevail upon Mr. Bolt to observe the law."

Dinah patted the man's hand. "I appreciate the offer, Oscar. But very frankly, I think that such an effort would be a waste of time and possibly even put your own life in serious danger. No, we must just stay here and wait until Clint returns."

"He does seem rather—how shall I put this, rather capable, does he not?"

"Yes, he is quite capable of defending himself. But not when so badly outnumbered."

"May I ask you a delicate question?"

Dinah looked directly at Oscar. "By all means, do so."

"Well, I have heard a rumor that our Mr. Adams was a lawman and a . . ."

Oscar could not get the last word out.

"A gunman? Is that what you heard?"

108

Oscar nodded. "Yes. Of course, I don't believe a word of it. The man is a complete gentleman and I'm sure he would never actually kill anyone unless in self defense."

Dinah explained very patiently. "Clint is widely known as the Gunsmith. And while the rumors are true, and he is a famous gunman, he would never kill anyone except in self defense or in the execution of his lawful duty. Be assured, Oscar, that Clint is a fine man and totally incapable of murder."

Oscar blinked. Dinah's admission seemed to have quite taken his words away. "I shall have to think about that," he said at last. "You see, I am a man who has devoted his entire life to the law and the court system of justice. To me, the only ones that reserve the right to execute are those that are ordered to do so by a court of law—and then only for the most heinous of crimes."

"Out in the west, we too strive to live by the law, but sometimes that is not possible," Dinah explained very carefully. "The law is either unable or unwilling to carry out its duty. Might then prevails and we call it the law of the gun."

"Then I am not sure I can be happy out here."

Dinah nodded. "Oscar, you must carefully decide that for yourself. I simply wanted to try and explain how things are different here. I don't want you to be shocked if. . . ." her words trailed away as she saw dust coming from the road leading to Piney.

"He's returning," Oscar said. "I told you that there would be no trouble."

But Dinah shook her head. "It's not him. Not alone anyway; there is too much dust."

She whirled and went inside for a moment. When she returned to the front porch, she had a Winchester rifle gripped tightly in her fists.

"My God!" Oscar wailed, staring at the rifle, "Surely you don't need that."

Dinah did not take her eyes off the body of riders who topped the hill and came thundering down toward her place. There could be no mistaking the huge outline of Abraham Bolt riding at the head of his men. And worse, he was not flanked by Johnny, the only man alive who had any control whatsoever on him.

"Oscar," she whispered. "Do me a favor. Please go and tell everyone to go inside their cabins and to remain in them until these men leave."

"But, I can't leave you here to face them alone!"

"Please, do as I say!" Dinah levered a shell into her rifle. The cold finality of that response sent Oscar bustling off toward the horseshoe players and all the other guests now staring at the approaching riders.

Dinah glanced out onto Mirror Lake and saw that her son and the fishermen were far out on the water and safe. She took a deep breath, knowing that she at least had that much to be grateful for. She watched the killer of her mother and father gallop onto her resort and a pen of laying hens flew into a squawking frenzy as the body of horsemen swept past.

She saw Oscar arguing with the horseshoe players and knew that there were many of them who would not like to go into their cabins. They weren't entirely easterners, but men of the west who understood the threat of physical danger and would not be easily intimidated by it. They were all successful men who had been tough and smart enough to win out against adversity. But they were old and civilized men, and therefore no help to her against the likes of Abraham Bolt.

Dinah squared her shoulders and waited. She wondered if they had already killed Clint Adams and if Abraham had decided it was now time to run her off. Let him try, she thought grimly, he will have to kill me first.

Chapter Twenty

Abraham raised one big hand as a signal and reined his horse up before the cabin. He stared at Dinah Morgan with unconcealed hatred and said, "Where's the Gunsmith hiding?"

Dinah prayed that her voice would not betray the fear she was trying to hide. "He's not here. He hasn't come back from Piney yet."

"You're lyin' to me, woman!" He twisted around in his saddle. "Some of you men go search the cabins! Look everywhere! I'll check her cabin myself."

"Hold it!" Dinah lifted her rifle to her shoulder, pointing it right at his heart. "I can't miss and I won't hesitate to kill you if you so much as put one foot on my land."

Abraham had his right boot over his cantle but now he eased it back into his stirrup. "You're bluffing," he hissed.

"If you believe that, why don't you just step down into the dirt and find out?"

She was not bluffing. She knew it and so did Abraham. The hate between them and their families ran too deep.

"If he's here . . . if you're hiding him, you're goin' to rue the day you were born," Abraham raged. "The

Gunsmith killed one of my men down in Piney and then he shot Johnny."

The rifle barrel trembled slightly, but Dinah held it targeted on the man's chest. She waited to hear how seriously Johnny had been wounded. She did not believe it could be too bad or Abraham would have come in shooting and nothing would have stopped him from exacting a terrible retribution.

"Johnny never even had a chance to defend himself against that killer and we're going to catch him and string the bastard up for a tall cottonwood!"

"You do what you will," Dinah said, her arms beginning to ache from holding the rifle trained on this man, "but get the hell off my land and stay off."

Abraham spat tobacco and it splattered against the hem of her dress. A tobacco stain could never be gotten rid of and Dinah knew the dress was ruined and that he knew it just as well. She had to force herself not to pull the trigger.

"This is all my land," Abraham said, twisting around in his saddle, one way and then the other so that he could see in a full circle about them. "Always was and still is."

"You're wrong," Dinah said. "My mother and father, they homesteaded it legal."

"They stole the sumbitch out from under me, damn you! I was here years before them. I killed grizzly and chopped trees down so to have meadows. I made this land and took care of it too! It's mine."

Dinah had heard this all before. "If you came to make a speech, you've done it. Now get off my land."

Abraham shook with bottled fury. "You're as stubborn and bullheaded as your mother and father, God rot their bodies! I won't let you keep this land and ruin it for everyone with a stream of goddamn tourists comin' in here all summer."

"You have no choice. I'm expanding. I'm staying. Now get out before I lose my patience and blow a hole in you!"

Abraham trembled. "I'll tell my boy what you said and how you didn't even ask about his health. I never will understand what the devil he saw in you except to screw you in the dirt like a damned Injun' squaw."

"Get out of here!" Dinah screamed, the rifle barrel shaking violently in her grasp.

Abraham laughed obscenely. He whirled his horse around and rode out slow. When he came abreast of Oscar and the horseshoe players who had refused to go inside, he reined up and glared down at them.

"You rich sumbitches best pack your bags and get the hell offa my land while you still are able to under your own steam. I'm comin' back some time soon and I'll burn out every stick of cabin on this place ground. And if any of you should try to stop us, you'll get a bullet and a shallow grave for your trouble."

His lip curled. "You better leave right now."

Oscar Marsh, pale as sandstone, jerkily moved a step forward and stammered, "You can't . . . can't threaten us that way. This is private property and. . . ."

But he didn't finish. Abraham Bolt slashed Oscar's round double-chinned face with his rawhide quirt. Oscar cried out in pain and fell back, blood rising to fire his cheeks and trickle down into his collar.

Dinah snapped. She took aim and fired but she was so upset her bullet went wide. The next instant, Abraham was spurring his men across the yard. Dinah did not have a clear shot and dared not risk hitting one of her own people.

When the riders disappeared over the hill, Dinah lurched around and went into the cabin. She closed and barred her door. She put the Winchester away very carefully and then she sat down at her small, homemade kitchen table, covered her mouth with her forearm, and began to cry with a mixture of rage and relief.

After a long time, she realized that there was a soft knocking at her door. "Are you all right, Miss Morgan?"

It was Oscar Marsh. She fought for control and angrily wiped her tears away. "Yes," she said. Then louder a second time. "Yes! I'm just fine, Oscar."

"The fishermen and your son must have heard the rifle shot because they are rowing fast on their way to the dock."

"Go tell them that everything is fine. Just fine. Tell them to please go back out on the lake and catch a big mess of trout for supper."

There was a long silence. Then Oscar said, "All right, Miss Morgan."

She remembered how surprised she had been when it had been Oscar, of all people, who had dared to stand up to Abraham Bolt and his riders. "Thank you very much," she said, coming up to the door but not yet wanting to open it because her face would be puffed and streaked with tears.

Dinah heard him whisper softly. "You're welcome."

And then she heard him walk away. Dinah took a deep breath and found a basin of water. She began to splash her face with its cool salve and wonder what had happened to Clint Adams and what would happen to all of them when Abraham Bolt returned.

Chapter Twenty-One

Dinah had tried to dispel the fear and apprehension by giving a sort of fish fry down beside her boat dock. She had asked Ben and Frank Hammer to clean their sacks of fish. Others had set the tables, worked in the kitchen and started the coals of their outdoor fire. The fish had tasted better than ever and everything had been perfect and yet . . . yet despite her best effort to bring an element of gaiety, the guests had been subdued and even fearful. One couple had even refused to go near the fire in case Abraham Bolt had ambushers hiding nearby.

It was awful the way this once happy and fun-loving crowd now was so morose, edgy and frightened. Dinah could not blame them. Abraham was a man who inspired fear, his size and appearance made him seem every bit as formidable as he really was. And he had threatened to kill the guests if they did not leave.

Dinah stood near the shore listening to the waves lap gently on the rocks. She could hear the guests talking quietly among themselves. Some had already decided to leave the resort and return home. Dinah could not blame them. It was hardly the sort of holiday they'd anticipated. This wasn't their resort or lake. They hadn't seen their parents die to keep this mountain paradise in their families.

They had no stake, but she had everything at stake including her son's future. And unless the fear that Abraham Bolt had instilled in these people was exorcised, Dinah knew that she would be financially ruined. She had invested everything and mortgaged her land to the hilt to begin the additional cabins. How ironic, she thought, that Abraham is about to win back his land without ever firing a shot or paying me one red cent. The land will be foreclosed upon and Abraham would make it known far and wide that he would tolerate no competing bidders for Mirror Lake. He would buy it for a fraction of its value.

A sharp argument broke out and Dinah could hear Oscar arguing with several other men. "There are laws to take care of this sort of situation," he said angrily. "No one can threaten to kill us."

"But Abraham Bolt sure did!"

"Then he is liable for assault which, in law, means the threat to do others harm. He can be sent to jail, even prison!"

"Ha! Fat lot of good that will do us when we are pushing up meadow grass! No, me and Portia are leaving for Los Angeles in the morning."

"We're going with you," another man said. "I feel awful, but we have to be prudent. We've been warned and Abraham Bolt is above the law on the Mogollon Rim."

Oscar angrily replied. "Nonsense! No man is above the law. Abraham Bolt is subject to the same laws as we are!"

"Not according to what I observed. The man rules up here, Oscar. Can't you understand that this is not some damned pampered class of would-be lawyers? For the law to mean anything, it has to be enforced and shown to work. That won't happen. Not in Piney, it won't!"

The Gunsmith had been listening from the trees. He had watched the people and waited to make sure that there were none of Bolt's men hidden close. Now, sure that there were not, he stepped out from hiding and said, "I think the law ought to be put to the test in Piney, don't you folks?"

His appearance startled everyone. The gathering fell silent and Dinah was snapped out of her own dark thoughts. She smiled and came to him with a hug that left no doubt about her feelings of happiness to see him safe and back again.

Clint held her for a moment. "It's going to be all right, Dinah," he whispered into her ear.

He turned to face the guests. "You'll all have to excuse me for eavesdropping. I just couldn't help but hear what was said and I agree with everyone. Oscar says no man is above the law—and he's right. Mr. Benedict and his lovely wife Portia feel very strongly that their lives are in danger. I agree with that too."

Clint had their undivided attention. He hooked his thumbs into his cartridge belt. "The thing of it is, Abraham Bolt wants me dead or at least off the Mogollon Rim. I shot one of his men and wounded his son—but in self defense. There were dozens of people on the street and if they have the courage to just testify to that truth, then I have nothing to worry about before any court of law."

"They'd never testify," Benedict said. "Not when they fear Abraham."

"I think you are very wrong. People know that they must stand up for their law or risk losing it and be at the mercy of the strongest. I have talked to Sheriff Gray, and he has agreed to protect me until a judge and jury can reach a verdict. The truth of what Bolt has done to intimidate and strike fear into everyone will be brought out."

"I will file a charge of assault and prosecute him to the limit," Oscar Marsh vowed. "No one can threaten our lives and not face punishment."

Clint frowned. He had not bargained for anyone else

to become the target of Abraham's considerable forces. "I don't think that is such a good idea."

"But I do! Don't you see? If you are willing to risk your neck proving that the system works, I have to do the same. We have both given much of our lives to law and order. In different ways, but still for the same belief in a system of justice and equality for all. I must test my own faith. You, Gunsmith, of all men I know, should be able to understand that."

Clint nodded. He understood perfectly. But that didn't mean he still didn't wish that Oscar would find a safer way to test his belief. Clint would be in jail and, therefore, completely unable to protect Oscar should Abraham go after him. And yet, he knew that Oscar would not back down or change his position.

"I hope," Clint finally said, "that if Oscar and I are willing to put our faith in the legal system, that you all put your faith in Dinah Morgan and what she is trying to do here. I have been privileged to get to know many of you. We've worked on these cabins side by side, caught a few fish, swapped a few jokes and become friends. I ask that you remain here and continue working at least as long as you originally planned to stay. I promise that, once I am in jail, there is no threat to you. If I lose my case, then leave. But not before. Not if you are individuals of courage and have faith in our system of justice."

"I'll stay," Benedict said after a long pause, "if Portia will."

"Sure I will!" the man's wife said.

In moments, the guests were voicing their support. Someone told a joke, and before long, everyone was chattering and laughing. Clint felt good about that. Now, Dinah had a chance again.

Chapter Twenty-Two

Clint had intended to leave for Piney that evening but the thought of spending such a beautiful night in jail filled him with dread. Clint had no idea how long it might take to get a trial, but Oscar Marsh had vowed to use a few connections in order to see that a federal judge was sent for immediately.

One by one, the couples left and Clint heard Dinah tell her son Ben to go turn in for the night. Clint stood beside the lake and watched the moon wash the water gold. Somewhere out in the lake a big fish splashed and Clint heard the hoot of an owl in the trees. He was going to hate being jailed and he wondered how it would feel to find himself on the wrong side of the bars after all these years. He also was thinking about the older couples that had walked hand in hand back to their cabins. One by one, their cabin lights had been snuffed out and Clint supposed that some of them were making love, holding each other and maybe reminiscing about their long marriages. It would be nice to marry some day, to find someone that would have him permanent.

Not that he was quite ready for that, however. There were still a few hills to climb, a few more ladies to be loved and new vistas to gallop Duke across, feeling as free and unfettered as a strong prairie wind. But when he ended his wandering days, Clint would not mind settling down with someone that he loved, liked, trusted and wanted to grow old holding every night.

He picked up a flat rock and sent it skipping over the water, golden spray scattered across the surface of the lake to form a succession of ripples.

"A penny for your thoughts, Clint."

He turned at the soft voice and saw Dinah standing behind him. "I must be getting old and hard of hearing to allow someone to come up behind me that way," he said, chiding himself for slipping into such an absorbing reverie. "I can't afford that."

She was wearing another dress, one without a tobacco-stained hem. It was pink and had puffy short sleeves and was cut low to reveal her full bosom. Her feet were bare and she wore a blue ribbon in her hair. She smelled of perfume, something that tasted like jasmine and Clint breathed deeply of her.

"What were you thinking?" she asked, coming up to stand almost against him in the soft moonlight.

"Nothing very important."

"I'll be the judge of that."

He chuckled softly. "All right. I was thinking about how I hoped that someday I would marry as fine and lovely a woman as you are, Dinah."

Her face glowed at the compliment. "Would you walk with me a little, Clint? After everything that happened today, I can't begin to think of sleep."

"It would be a pleasure." She gave him her hand and they walked along the shore, hearing the croaking of frogs. Clint hoped they would walk all night. He did not want to think about tomorrow and the days he'd soon be spending in jail. He would use this evening to think of during that time and it would make his waiting a little easier.

"Come this way," she said, pulling him from the shore and entering the meadow. She stopped and turned to him.

Something in her eyes, and the way her lips parted softly made his pulse quicken with anticipation and when she came into his arms, it felt natural and right. They kissed, softly at first, then with growing passion and urgency.

Dinah tore her lips from his and whispered, "Please make love to me right here and now, Clint."

"With pleasure."

She turned and he unbuttoned her dress and when she pivoted around, it fell from her shoulders and he saw that she had wanted him from the beginning because she wore nothing underneath. He bent and his lips brushed across her chest and then worked their way down to her nipples.

"Oh, God," she breathed, "it has been so very long since a man did this to me."

He sucked one breast, then the other, back and forth, delighted with their firmness and size. Her breath came faster and faster and he could feel her legs begin to tremble.

"Stop," she begged softly.

Clint pulled back and she kissed him with fierce urgency, then unbuttoned his shirt and began to suck on his nipples. It was crazy, but it fired his blood and made his cock grow long and hard. She began to unbuckle his pants after first helping him remove his gun and holster. His breath drew in sharply when one of her hands found his manhood and the other pushed his pants down.

She stepped back and stared down at him. "You are huge, Clint," she said with unconcealed admiration.

She slipped out of her dress to stand before him completely naked. With both hands on his cock, she stepped in close and spread her feet wide apart. Then, she began to rub him up and down against her until she was slick and wet.

"How does it feel?" he asked, loving what she was doing but feeling his hips begin to rock back and forth with eagerness.

"I'm surprised you need to ask." She hunched her hips down and then up and groaned to feel him enter her at last. She was soaking wet and very ready for him. Her hips began to move back and forth and he quickly matched her thrusting rhythm.

Her mouth sought his as their bodies lunged back and forth with a quickening pace. They tumbled to the ground. As Dinah landed on him she cried, "Oh, Clint, it's in so far now! Yes!" she cried as he drove into her all the way and began to piston joyously.

"Do it to me! Don't stop, don't . . . . . ahhhh yes!"

When she came, she was a woman possessed with passion that took all of him and gloried in squeezing his manhood for every drop of his spewing sperm. She gripped his buttocks and bit his neck, then raked his back almost hard enough to draw blood. She could not seem to stop bucking under him and Clint could not stop filling her hot womanhood.

Afterward, they lay silently for a long time in the meadow. They stared up at the stars and saw one shoot across the heavens and disappear forever.

"I love you," she whispered. "No one has ever done what you are doing to save me."

"You mean going to jail?"

"Yes."

"I'm doing it for all of us, Dinah. And for Ben, too. I want you to make it here. To have the finest resort in the west. You can and will if we beat Abraham Bolt."

"With you I will."

He rolled over to face her. "Besides, even though you may think you love me, I'm not your man. Johnny is."

She closed her eyes and tears squeezed out of them. "How did you know I loved him too?"

"It's pretty obvious. I don't think either of you have fooled very many people—at least about that part of it."

She opened her eyes. "What is that supposed to mean?"

"Just this," he said. "When Johnny came to be with you in Boston you conceived Ben. Ben is Johnny's son, not your late husband's."

"That's not true!"

"Yes it is. I'm not exactly sure how you fooled everyone. But my guess is that Johnny is about a year or eighteen months older than you've told people. He's six, not five. And from what I pieced together, your late husband was a small man. Ben is going to be over six feet tall—just like his real father. Admit it, Dinah."

"For what purpose!" she cried, pushing him back and climbing to her feet. "So that old Abraham could laugh and prove that I was a whore? That Ben is a bastard? What good!"

Clint stepped up to her and drew her close. After their lovemaking, their scents had become one—musky and strong. "Maybe you're right," he said quietly. "At any rate, I would never tell anyone. I swear that."

She sagged against him with relief. After a moment, she kissed him quickly and took his hand. "Let's go for a swim. I'm hot and sticky."

"The water is pretty cold," he hedged.

"I know. It'll stimulate you, Clint. And then after our swim, we can get hot and sticky together all over again!"

Clint swallowed. Studied that lovely hunk of woman that was going to be his tonight as much and as often as he could take. How could a man refuse someone like her?

He followed Dinah's swaying buttocks down to the water and went in after her.

Chapter Twenty-Three

Dinah, Ben and Oscar drove Clint off to Piney the next morning. Duke would be far happier left out by Mirror Lake with Dinah's other horses.

"I hope you're doing the right thing," Dinah fussed, sitting very close to him, her face worried but her cheeks still a little flushed from their long and exciting night of lovemaking. "Once in that jail, you'll be all but helpless."

Clint was driving and his eyes dropped to his boot top. He had a two-shot derringer tucked inside along with several extra bullets. In his other boot, he had a knife and a lockpick that he knew would open any country jail cell without much work. "You have to remember, Dinah, I'm turning myself in to make a point, not only to your guests, but also to the people in town. If they see that justice is done, I think that they'll finally understand that Abraham Bolt can be made to abide by the law."

"And if you fail, you might go to prison. Isn't it true that an ex-lawman would be a dead man in a prison?"

"I've never put much thought to that," Clint said. "If I were sentenced to prison for killing a man in self defense, I think I'd break free and find some new real estate to explore."

Oscar was especially quiet in the second seat with

Ben. Clint hoped and expected the man had changed his mind about filing charges against Abraham. But Oscar was still determined to take Abraham to trial.

"I'll file assault charges at once and then take that mail coach down to Phoenix this afternoon. From there, I can go to the territorial offices. I don't trust Bolt and, if I'm successful, I'll be back in two days with a United States Marshal and a circuit judge."

"I'd appreciate that," Clint said. "Last thing I want is to cool my heels in a jail cell for a couple of weeks."

"I know you may not believe this," Oscar said quietly, "but I have many friends in high places who owe this old law professor a few favors."

That made everyone feel much better. Oscar might be a little naive and idealistic about what the law could and could not do on the frontier, but he was not a man who made empty promises.

"How long will the trial last?" Clint asked.

"Yours or the one I am pressing for against Abraham Bolt?"

"Mine."

"Two days at the most. All we need to do is to find the witnesses you spoke of and get their testimony." Oscar cleared his throat. "Dinah, that has to be your job. You know these people and stand the best chance of convincing them to step forward."

"I'll find them and make sure they testify," she promised. "Just make sure that you get that federal marshal and judge up here as soon as possible. Until they arrive, Clint's life is in danger."

"I'm acutely aware of that fact," the law professor said. "Before seeing Abraham Bolt and his men ride in, I assumed that the law was supreme here. It isn't. This has caused me a great deal of consternation but I had to be honest enough to admit the truth. And, Clint, if anything should happen to you before . . ."

"Hold up, Oscar!" Clint said, half laughing but also

half serious. "I'm called the Gunsmith and while I've never particularly liked that nickname, it's mine because I've gotten out of a lot worse fixes than I'm heading for now. I've learned to count mostly on myself and I don't say that because I don't believe you can't deliver. All I'm trying to tell you is that I can and will take care of myself no matter what happens."

Ben clapped his hands together and cried. "You'd shoot that old Abraham dead and all his men too, wouldn't ya, Gunsmith!"

Clint twisted around on his driver's seat and smiled at the boy. The fact that they were speaking about shooting the boy's real grandfather seemed painfully ironic. "I would if it was my life or theirs, son. But we're going to let a judge and jury decide what's fair. That's the way it ought to be and why we have laws in this country."

Oscar Marsh beamed. "The Gunsmith is a very good man, Ben. You'll notice he's not even wearing his sidearm."

Clint touched his finger to his lips. Oscar didn't see it but Ben did and the boy kept his secret about the weapons in Clint's boottops.

"Normally," Sheriff Gray said, "I search my prisoners, but I'll make any exception in your case, Gunsmith."

"Good idea." Clint would not have submitted to a search.

The iron door clanged shut behind Clint and he would have been lying to himself not to admit that it made the hair along the back of his neck prickle.

After a few more minutes, when it became obvious that there was nothing more to say, Dinah, Ben and Oscar Marsh left.

Alone now, Clint studied his cell with a professional's interest. The walls were solid rock and mortar. The roof was fifteen feet high and looked solid; the floor was rock just like the wall. The cell itself smelled strongly of soap and lye and Clint realized that the sheriff must have had it scrubbed and mopped out especially for his famous guest. Clint appreciated that because now, the cell was cleaner than the rest of the office.

It had one bed and a lumpy straw mattress, no pillow. There was a chamber pot and a tin of water sitting on a small table with one broken leg wired together. Light streamed in from an alley window and when Clint stood on his tiptoes, he could just see outside. The bars were very solidly imbedded in the rock and mortar. They did not look like they could be pulled out with anything less than a team of six or eight mules.

"Your friend is makin' a damn big mistake by filing charges of assault against Mr. Bolt. I sure wish you'd have talked him out of that, Gunsmith," the sheriff said with a sad shake of his head.

Clint turned back to look through the bars into the office. Sheriff Gray was seated at his desk, feet up, smoking a cigarette.

"I tried," Clint answered. "But Abraham has to learn the hard way that he can't threaten to shoot everyone who disagrees with him."

"You hear the threat?"

"Nope. But practically everyone else out at Dinah's Place did. They'll testify."

"Maybe, maybe not. Bunch of old rich folks. I doubt they want any trouble." Sheriff Gray stood up and stretched. He consulted his pocket watch and then sauntered to the door. "It's noontime and that means it's time to eat. I'll bring you back something."

"Thanks." Clint watched him lock the front door and leave. The office brooded in silence and Clint paced aimlessly around in a circle. He hadn't gotten much sleep the night before out in the meadow with Dinah.

Not that he was complaining. Hell no. But a man did need to sleep.

Clint stretched out on the lumpy mattress and pulled his stetson over his eyes. He fell asleep hoping that Sheriff Gray would bring him back something decent to eat.

Sheriff Gray did not go straight to lunch but instead he angled around behind town and stepped into the woods. He pulled out a paper and stub of pencil and began to labor over a long note. When it was finally written, he pulled a rusted tobacco can out of a fallen log, inserted the message and then pushed the can back into its secret hiding place. The sheriff rolled another cigarette, lit it and strolled on back to town feeling hungry enough to eat a horse.

Less than twenty minutes later, one of Abraham's men was galloping toward the Bolt Ranch with the secret message. And within another hour, six mounted riders were heading to intercept the mail coach that would carry Oscar Marsh on his way to Phoenix, a judge and a marshal.

It seemed rather straight forward to Abraham—eliminate Oscar Marsh and you killed all interference. It also solved the little problem of going to trial for threatening those damned guests out at Dinah's Place. The fat little law professor was the only one among all the guests who would press charges and then mount any kind of a prosecution.

Abraham figured it was as easy as shooting fish in a rain barrel.

Chapter Twenty-Four

Oscar Marsh clung to the front seat of a buckboard and tried not to look down at the ravine on his side of the narrow, mountain road. He was a nervous wreck after only one hour of this hairraising experience and they still had a good five thousand more feet to drop until they were on the desert floor and could race toward Phoenix. Oscar had never experienced anything like this ride and vowed that he never would again.

The mail coach driver was a wizened, tobacco-spitting monkey with forearms like thick tree roots and a mouth filthier than a sewer. He drove without seeming to look at the road. He would not deign to slow for any of the seemingly endless series of loops, hairpin curves and even switchbacks. Sometimes, the mail wagon would actually raise up on one side and then Oscar would utter a fervent prayer and close his eyes. He was certain that the immense centrifical force would hurl the wagon over the mountain's edge where it would disintegrate on the great rocks below. But each time, the wagon miraculously righted itself on all four wheels. It slammed down with such force that it seemed to drive Oscar's spine up through his cranium.

"Hell of a nice day, ain't it," the driver, whose name Oscar had momentarily forgotten due to a mental paralysis born of craven fear, yelled. "Hell of a nice day!"

"I'd enjoy it far more, sir, if you would slow down a little!"

"Ahh, don't worry professor, I been driving this road in good weather and bad for almost ten years and we ain't spilled over yet. Hell, you should see how much fun I have when the road is covered with snow and ice!"

"It's an experience I shall definitely forego."

"Haa! I like your sense of humor, professor! Who ever said you egg-headed bastards all got your heads up your ass so's you never smile or crack a joke!"

Oscar winced at the crude image and hung on tight as the buckboard slithered around another sharp curve and momentarily hung balanced like a spinning top. Rock and gravel sprayed out over the edge of a monstrous cliff and dropped four hundred feet to a river gorge below. Oscar felt like his chest was being crushed and his poor heart was going to explode with terror.

"Lean a little."

"What!"

"I said you oughta lean a little toward me and that way you'd be less likely to be tossed over the side."

Oscar leaned.

"What you going to do in Phoenix?"

"Be bedridden for six months if I survive this mountain!" Oscar yelled. "Please slow down! There's a very sharp curve up ahead!"

"Hell," the driver said, spitting tobacco and striking a favorite rock dead center, "I know that!"

They did have to slow for the curve a little, and when they came out of it, the driver let the horses run again so that Oscar found themselves right back up to the same terrifying speed. God have mercy, he thought, wishing he could mop the sweat and fear off of his face but not daring to pry his fingers loose.

After this ride, Abraham Bolt held no fear for him, none at all. He saw another curve up ahead and closed his eyes remembering he needed to lean. He felt the iron rims of the buckboard trying to bite into the earth but instead skidding sideways. Gravel pelleted the underside of the buckboard and when Oscar peeked he saw the mountainside sweeping downward at at least a seventy degree angle. Hundreds of feet below, the wild river beat at a gorge that held it like a chained animal.

Ten years, Oscar told himself over and over. Three times a week for ten years and never tipped over. Hang on!

He did not hear the rifle shots, only the driver when he bellowed in rage and tried to grab the brake handle. But there was no chance at all. Both horses were hit in the neck and began to fall. The poor beasts ran dead on their feet for maybe twenty yards and then they crashed into a tangled pile. The buckboard struck their bodies and Oscar felt himself being slingshotted into the sky. He heard the driver screaming and opened his eyes to see the man dropping like a stone to carom off a boulder and go whirling down toward the gorge below. Oscar had never seen a dead man, but he knew by the way the man's body whirled that all the life had been battered from it.

Oscar smashed off a rock and lost consciousness. In a maelstrom of spinning pain he felt himself being slammed against rock and trees. His flesh was shredded by spiny plants and brush and he kept spinning faster and faster until he felt nothing but confused motion that carried him deeper into a black funnel of nothingness.

He awoke in a fog of pain and tried to lose himself again but failed. There were voices and for a joyous moment of madness, he thought they were angels calling him up to heaven. Stupid man, he railed from within, they are killers. They want to make sure you are dead but are afraid to come down this far and put a bullet into your thick, bleeding skull.

Oscar discarded that first impulse to raise his head and feebly cry out for help. He lay very, very still. He could hear the rushing river close by and he knew that his feet were lower than his head. But that was all he knew for sure, that, and that he was sticky with his own blood.

The voices called for a long time and when they finally vanished, Oscar dared to open his eyes and look around. All he saw was rocks and bushes. Then, he saw pieces of the wagon and . . . and yes, the ripped body of the driver and the foreleg of one horse that had been torn off against the base of a thick tree.

Oscar tried to move and could not. He wanted to cry but could not do that either. I am going to die here and that is that, he thought. Somehow, the idea did not seem so terrible. But then he remembered the reason he was here was because someone had shot the horses. And that someone had to be Abraham Bolt who needed to prevent him from reaching Phoenix alive. And the reason to do that was very simple—Abraham did not want Clint Adams to have a fair trial or a marshal to protect him from harm. Everything would then fit for Abraham Bolt and he would have ruthlessly won the game. He would also have proved conclusively that there was no law after all on the Mogollon Rim.

"But there is a law, and it is everywhere in America!" Oscar choked. His fingers dug into the rocky ground and he tried to pull himself upward toward the road far above.

It was hopeless. He was too old, fat and weak. Then I must go down, he thought, to water. Maybe I can just survive until I am found. Someone will come. Someone will investigate the accident and I will call out to them and they will help.

But who would come? And how would they ever find

him? Wouldn't the men Abraham sent wipe out all visible trace of the accident? Certainly! Oscar swallowed a rock of bitterness. I must not think of that, he decided. I must simply stay alive.

Hope and a system of law were alike that way, they both existed until the last man gave them up.

Chapter Twenty-Five

Clint heard angry shouting out in the street. Then the door began to shake under the impact of closed fists. It was a lynch mob and they were calling Clint's name. He knew it as sure as he knew that the mob would have been liquored up on Abraham Bolt's money.

Clint was on his feet instantly. In all his years of being a sheriff, he had only heard the cries of a lynch mob three times but each time the sound had been unforgettable. A crowd of kill-crazed men was the worst form of humanity and it was always led by a few blustering cowards. Men who had an axe to grind but needed the strength of numbers to get an enemy hanged.

Clint hated lynch mobs. He had never allowed one to get up to his office door, not like the men outside hammering against this office. Very early in his illustrious law career, Clint had decided that the best way to deal with a lynch mob was to strike at its leaders hard and fast. Make them reveal their yellow stripe right away and humiliate them to leave them weak and ashamed. It was absolutely fatal to waver, show even the slightest hint of indecision or let them think you might be bullied.

Sheriff Gray bolted out of his chair and he started hesitantly for the door.

"No!" Clint bellowed. "Grab your shotgun and let

133

them know you mean business!''

"My shotgun? Hell, those boys outside are the people I grew up with. They're my friends." The man shook his head stubbornly. "I couldn't open fire on them."

"Dammit," Clint swore with exasperation, "you took an oath of office to protect your prisoners! Being a lawman isn't any popularity contest. Grab the shotgun!''

But the sheriff's mind was made up. "Nope. I'll do whatever I can to persuade them to stop their liquorin' it up and to go home and go to sleep. But I won't even make a show of acting like I'd open fire on 'em with a shotgun."

"They're drunk! Don't you see? Abraham Bolt has paid them to lynch me. You won't reason with anyone. All that's going to happen is that I'll get strung up and goddamnit, I won't let that happen!"

The sheriff shrugged his shoulders. "I heard tell you have killed a lot of men, Gunsmith. I believe that a few of them were innocent men that did not deserve to die. Maybe it's time you paid the piper. Huh?"

The sheriff smiled wickedly and if Clint had any last doubts about who the man was loyal to, those doubts were now completely dispelled—the sheriff worked for Abraham Bolt and he was selling Clint out to a lynch mob.

Clint had no choice. He reached down into his boot and pulled out the derringer and cocked its hammer. "Touch the door and you are a dead man. This little bulldog in my fist packs a .44 caliber bullet and I can't miss at this range."

The sheriff wanted to draw, but he knew that the Gunsmith was as good as his word. Sheriff Gray pulled his hand away from his gun but he was livid with anger. "You sonofabitch, I knew I should have searched you."

"I would have killed you first. Now, turn around slow and put your hands straight out from your sides. Grab those keys from the peg, and open this cell fast."

"You'll never make it out of here. There's no way except the front door. When that mob outside learns you are holding a gun, they'll burn this building and both of us in it right down to the foundation."

"That just means that if I go, so do you. Now, do as I say and hurry up!"

The sheriff did as he was told but Clint could tell the man was dragging his heels. When he finally opened the cell, Clint could see the front door of the office beginning to split from the hard pounding it was taking by the mob.

Clint disarmed the sheriff then grabbed him by the throat and shoved him back across the room. "I'm going to give you a little lesson in mob control whether you like it or not."

Clint grabbed a Winchester rifle and levered a shell, then pointed it high up on the door and blew a hole through it. He heard shouts and then a few running feet. After a second, the pounding started again and this time he leveled the rifle at the door and fired. The slug ripped through wood and they both heard a high-pitched scream.

"Jesus Christ, Floyd has been shot. Clear out of here! Get back!"

Clint grabbed a double barreled shotgun and broke it to see that it was loaded. He thumbed back the hammers and hissed, "Unlock the door and step out quick. Turn right and keep moving fast. If anybody yells for you to stop, you'd better ignore them or you're a dead man. You are going to find us two fast horses and we're going for a long, hard ride."

The sheriff shook his head back and forth. "I can't do this! Bolt will think I betrayed him. He'll kill me for sure."

"And I'll kill you if you don't do what I say. You've got only one chance to live and that's to help get me out of this town safe. Do that, and I won't shoot you—

though I sure ought to for setting me up for a lynch mob's rope.''

Clint jammed the shotgun into the man's spine hard and warned, ''Mess up, and I'll blow you all across a storefront. Understand?''

Sheriff Gray nodded. His face was waxen, his eyes dilated and blinking like frightened, trapped things. Clint had no doubt at all that the man would do exactly as he was ordered.

The bolt lock slid open and the sheriff said in a crushed voice, ''What if they start firing at us the minute the door opens?''

''Then they'll hit you because I'm going to be right behind you all the way.''

Clint had to grab the doorknob and turn it himself the sheriff was so frozen with terror. He kicked the door open and shoved the man out. Someone yelled for them to stop but Clint was pushing the sheriff along fast.

A gun fired and a bullet bit wood splinters near their faces. ''Run,'' Clint shouted. ''Take the first alley we come to and move!''

Sheriff Gray did not need any urging. He was old and out of shape but when a second slug blew his hat from his head, the sheriff sprinted off like a deer.

When they ran, the crowd snapped out of its confusion and began to fire. Clint heard the sheriff grunt with pain and saw him grab his upper arm. But the man was so afraid he did not even miss stride. It seemed as if they ran a mile-long gauntlet of fiery lead until they finally came to the first side alley. In fact, they probably did not cover twenty-five yards.

''This way!'' the sheriff cried hoarsely. ''We'll find some horses down here!''

Clint blasted through one alley and then they were racing along a back street with the sound of the angry mob close behind. A big dog burst out of a yard and sank its fangs in the sheriff's leg but his boottop saved him from a serious wound. Clint kicked the dog away and it rolled howling. Someone shouted in anger and a door slammed.

Suddenly, gunshots sounded behind them and when Clint glanced over his left shoulder, he saw the mob coming. Most of them were too drunk to run fast, but a few of Abraham's gunmen were sober and determined to gun them down.

They rounded another corner and there wasn't a single tied horse on the road. The sheriff staggered and fell. "Go on without me!" he begged.

The crowd was coming fast. Clint saw another alley just ahead and he hauled the sheriff to his feet. "Like hell I will!" he spat. "You're the key to bringing Abraham Bolt down and you're going to sing like a bird."

A bullet cut through Clint's shirt and he felt the raw sting of torn flesh across his ribs. But he had the sheriff back on his feet and moving again. The alley ahead was dark. Maybe they could get lost in this night and somehow escape. But right now, it didn't seem like the kind of thing to bet on.

Chapter Twenty-Six

They shook off most of their pursuers, but not all of them. One man in particular was especially fast. Every three or four strides, Clint would glance back and see the man closing the gap between them a foot or two at each stride. Clint thought about abandoning the sheriff who was slowing him down. He rejected the idea. The sheriff would know everything about Abraham Bolt, he had to be the key to the powerful rancher's downfall.

I've got to keep him alive, Clint thought.

The man behind them fired and his bullet drilled the sheriff's empty, flapping holster and ripped it from his cartridge belt. There was no doubt that the next bullet would hit one or the other of them square in the back. Clint slid to a stop, rolled and jammed the shotgun to his shoulder. He fired without really even taking aim and the speedy foot racer was suddenly hurled away like a child's doll during a temper tantrum. Tight-faced, Clint climbed back to his feet, then twisted and raced to catch up with the sheriff.

"Where are some horses!"

"I . . . I thought . . . there be some tied along . . . . here!"

Clint could see that the man was beginning to stagger. Breath was tearing in and out of his lungs and even terror could not drive his body much farther.

"Turn right!" Clint shouted, grabbing the man and turning him back toward the main street of town.

"But . . . but they'll find us . . . for dead certain!"

Maybe, Clint thought, but they had about reached the edge of town and the last thing he wanted to do was to race into the forest on foot. Men on horses would quickly encircle them and by daybreak they would be cornered like rabbits and either shot or hanged.

"Not if we grab some horses first," Clint said raggedly.

They stumbled along the side street and just as they neared the main road through town, Clint heard the sound of galloping horses approaching.

Clint tackled the sheriff cleanly, then grabbed the man and rolled in close to a thick hedge in a desperate attempt to avoid being seen by the riders. The sheriff clawed at his throat and started to shout a warning. Clint filled the man's mouth with his fist and the warning cry ended with a muffled whimper.

"Shoot them on sight! Both of them!" Abraham Bolt roared as he swept by on horseback moving in the same direction that they'd been running. "I want them both dead!"

The riders thundered past not ten feet from the hedge where Clint lay pressed to the earth with his hand clamped firmly over Sheriff Gray's broken lips. When the riders passed, Clint stood up and hauled the exhausted sheriff to his feet. The shotgun was too much of a giveaway on main street so he poked it into the shrubbery. Clint pulled their hats low over their faces and then drapped his left arm over the sheriff's shoulders as they staggered back into the center of town looking like a pair of drunken cowboys.

They passed running, shouting men and were heading straight for a pair of unattended horses when Clint happened to notice how the lamplight gleamed dully off the sheriff's tarnished badge. He made a grab for it but he was too late. Two men coming their way stopped right in front of Clint and their faces did a doubletake.

"Hey," one of them began, "You're...."

Clint attacked wishing he still had the shotgun to use as a club. Instead, all he had was his fists and he used them knowing his life depended on how successful he was in killing any cry of warning.

His first, desperate punch landed squarely against one of the men's throat. The blow paralyzed the man's voice box and dropped him gagging to the ground. The second man had an extra half-second but Clint brought his knee up into his groin and doubled him with pain. He grabbed him by the collar and propelled him headfirst into a storefront wall and the man dropped and did not move again.

Clint shoved the nearly incapacitated sheriff at the nearest horse.

"Mount up or I'll shoot you where you stand!" Clint hissed.

The sheriff lifted his head and began to shake it. Clint poked him in the face with the derringer and the sheriff spun around and fought his way onto the waiting horse.

Clint tore the reins from the hitch rail and, together, he and the sheriff of Piney spurred out of town the opposite way that Abraham and his riders had gone.

With the wind in his face and with no immediate threat of being killed or lynched, Clint suddenly felt a whole lot better. There was a nearly full moon and the road was easy to follow. He knew that he could not go back to Dinah's Place but instead needed to use the sheriff against their enemies.

Clint thought of Oscar Marsh and how the man had said he had many important friends in Phoenix. That was their only hope—Phoenix. There, Clint figured he could get the sheriff to tell the truth about what had really happened tonight and about how Abraham operated.

Yes, he thought, angling for the mountain road that would take him off of this mountain. He would find Oscar and before Sheriff Gray was through singing his tale, there would be a warrant for Abraham Bolt's arrest.

Hang on, Dinah, he thought, just give me another day or two and Oscar and I will have this whole thing wrapped up as neat as a catalogue store order.

Clint glanced up at the bright moon. Tonight, there was going to be a lot of hell raising on the Mogollon Rim.

Chapter Twenty-Seven

Clint and the sheriff moved at a fast, ground-eating trot along the narrow road leading down off the Mogollon Rim. The road was a twisting snake, with steep dropoffs plummeting to a brush-choked gorge far below. Clint wished they were on flat ground where they could move faster, but there was no help for that so he tried to content himself with their progress.

He studied the stars above and wondered how long it would take to reach Phoenix and if, when he returned, Dinah and her guests would still be alive. Maybe, he thought, I should just turn around and go back to Mirror Lake and be ready when Abraham and his men come—as they surely will. What good is getting help from Phoenix going to do after Abraham destroys Dinah's Place?

Clint was weighing the need to protect Dinah Morgan against the fact that Sheriff Gray was the key to breaking the rule of Abraham Bolt. If he could just get this corrupt lawman to. . . .

Their galloping horses shied so violently that both Clint and the sheriff were almost unseated. One minute they were traveling down the mountainside, the next their animals were rearing and fighting in wide-eyed terror.

"Whoa!" Clint yelled, fighting to get the crazed

horse under control. "Easy!"

The sheriff was also talking to his animal, trying to calm it. "What the hell is wrong with these jugheads!" he demanded.

"Damned if I know." Clint got his horse faced ahead. He whipped it smartly across the hindquarters but the spooked animal snorted and refused to go ahead. Forefeet planted far apart, eyes rolling with terror, it shivered and balked.

"Let's dismount and see what's got these horses so rattled," Clint said, stepping down and handing his reins to the sheriff.

Clint saw nothing at first, but he kept on studying the road because something sure had to be amiss. Then, he knelt and studied the ground very closely. There was enough moonlight to see where the earth was dark and crusted. Someone had tried to cover it up with more dirt, but it hadn't worked. He scraped the crusted material with his fingernail and lifted it to his nostrils. Still not sure, he touched it with his tongue and then crumbled it between his fingers.

Blood.

Clint stood up slowly. A lot of blood. More than could have leaked out of a man. Horses. Clint realized that a horse had been shot here, maybe more than one horse and that explained why their saddlehorses were so panicked.

"Well, what is it?" the sheriff demanded sullenly.

Clint felt no obligation to reply yet. He walked over to the edge of the road and peered down into the gorge below. The river's roar filled his ears and he could taste its spray. But those things were suddenly forgotten when he noticed how moonlight glinted against a piece of metal and then he saw, way down and almost hidden in the tangle of brush, the outline of a shattered wagon. Clint knew that the wrecked wagon might have been lying down there in the gorge for years, but somehow, that did not seem likely. Not with blood fresh enough to terrorize their saddlehorses still on the road.

Clint felt his stomach suck in with dread. He turned around and said, "Sheriff, we're going to do a little investigation. Untie the ropes and get your legs together because we have some climbing ahead of us."

"What the hell do you mean?"

Clint told him and finished by saying, "If Oscar Marsh and the driver have been murdered, I'm going to put the blame squarely on your shoulders."

"I had nothing to do with this!"

"You must have known it would happen."

"Prove it!"

Clint grabbed the man by the shirtfront. He would have liked nothing better than to shove him over the edge and watch him ricochet from rock to rock all the way down to the bottom. Instead, he shoved him ahead. "We tie the horses here and start down."

"You're crazy! We can't go down there in the dark!"

"We've the moonlight. Let's go, you first."

The sheriff wanted to refuse but when he studied Clint's face, he changed his mind and started on down.

The going was treacherous because the side of the mountain was covered with loose shale. Time after time they both slipped and fell, then almost gathered momentum and began a roll that would have sent them tumbling all the way to the river. They reached the ends of their ropes and kept moving downward.

"We'll never get back up again!" the sheriff cried. "We could die down here!"

"If you don't shut up, you're going to die right now," Clint warned. "Keep moving!"

Clint cupped his hands and shouted against the roar of the river. "Oscar!"

Oscar Marsh heard the shout. He opened his eyes and listened, afraid that the men who had killed the driver and wanted to kill him had suddenly returned. If they had, Oscar was determined to make them work to find him. He would not make it easy for a gang of murderers by giving them his position and a good target.

"Oscar, are you down there! It's me, Clint Adams. The Gunsmith!"

Oscar blinked. A smile creased his round, battered and very scratched face. He pushed himself up from beside the river. "Yes!" he shouted.

Clint stopped. He was still a good hundred yards from the bottom of the gorge and it was very hard to hear anything because of the roaring white water. But he had heard something.

"Come on!" he said impatiently to the sheriff who had fallen so many times he was covered with dirt and stickers.

"No man could have gone over this and lived. Give up! We're already in too far."

But Clint ignored the man. He was sliding and moving down faster, burying his heels into the loose gravel and shale, ignoring the burning sensation in his legs.

"Clint, help!"

The Gunsmith stopped. Strained to listened. Now he heard Oscar's feeble cry. It echoed faintly along the walls of the gorge. Clint forgot about the sheriff and hurried on down to find the law professor. And the dark pessimism he had been experiencing a few hours ago vanished. Now, all he had to do was try and get the man to Phoenix and help.

"Are you all right?" he asked, kneeling beside the law professor.

"Quite," the man assured him. "I can't tell you how relieved I am to see you, Clint."

"No broken bones?"

"No, but I'm so sore I can hardly move. And famished."

Clint nodded. The man looked drawn. "We'll get you out of here."

Oscar started to say something but the words died in his mouth.

The silent warning sent Clint spinning around and he saw Sheriff Gray. The man had picked up a massive rock and had it held high overhead. He was only ten feet above Clint and now he grunted as he threw the rock.

Clint tried to throw himself sideways but the footing was so loose he slipped and the rock crashed against his shoulder and knocked him into the river.

The rushing water tore at him and he floundered, trying to grab something. Oscar yelped and Clint glanced up to see the law professor backing up as the sheriff hurled another rock at him. Then, Oscar jumped into the river with Clint.

The water tore at them and the sheriff was grabbing more rocks and trying to brain them. Clint ducked one rock. He scrambled for footing, found none and grabbed Oscar. Together, they allowed themselves to be swept down the murderous gorge.

Chapter Twenty-Eight

The ice cold water churned savagely down through the narrow defile of rocks. Clint had all he could do just to keep his head above water and they had not gone twenty yards before it became apparent that Oscar Marsh could not swim. The man was thrashing in blind terror and the roar of the river made communication all but impossible.

Clint caromed off a rock and almost lost his grip on the law professor. He heard the roaring river grow stronger and even though the moonlight was poor down in this canyon, Clint knew that they were quickly approaching a waterfall. Clint shouted and pulled hard for the shore, and his one free hand clawed for anything to stop their forward momentum. He raked low hanging branches and tore his fingertips bloody but the force of the current was too strong and he could not hold on without releasing Oscar to drown.

Just before the waterfall the Gunsmith saw a log caught and wedged between two rocks. The log was about a foot above the water and appeared solid. Clint knew they had to grab it and pull themselves up or they were doomed. They could not survive *any* kind of waterfall. There was so much power and white water that they'd be bashed into unconsciousness before they were torn entirely to pieces on the rocks below.

"Oscar," he screamed, "grab that log!"

The man looked half-drowned and almost helpless. He was still splashing, but only feebly. "Oscar! Grab the log!"

Oscar opened his eyes and peered into the darkness. He seemed to understand. He had better, Clint thought, as they hurled forward toward the waterfall.

Clint had to let go of Oscar at the very last instant or he would have been destroyed. Oscar understood this and when they were only a second away from being swept under the log, Oscar somehow found the strength to heave his arms and body out of the river, looking like a walrus flopping onto an ice floe. Clint did the same and they both slammed into the log, knocking the wind from their lungs. Clint felt the lower part of his body snap under the log as the swift current tried to pull him under. He dug his bloody fingers into the mushy bark and hauled himself up to safety inch by agonizing inch.

"Hang on!" Clint shouted, straddling the log and pulling Oscar up by the shirt and anything else he could grab. The man was very heavy and Clint's hard body strained until his muscles quivered. At last, Oscar was on top of the log. Face pressed to the bark, pale, coughing up water—but alive.

The gorge was cold, the spray from the waterfall bone-chilling. Now Clint could see that the falls dropped about twenty-five feet and the water must have crashed over big boulders because the sound of it was awesome.

"We have to move," Clint shouted. "We need to get to shore and start moving."

"I can't," Oscar groaned. "I'm finished."

"No you're not!" Clint began to crab his way across the rock-bound log, thanking every blessed inch of it for saving their lives.

He reached the shore and dragged himself painfully through a tangle of mossy boulders, then climbed up to a point of safety. He was not surprised when Oscar came grunting and wheezing along shortly after. Clint studied the man closely, trying to gauge if he had enough stamina and strength to climb out of this trap. The answer was no.

Clint pushed himself up to his feet. To remain down in this gorge was to die. He needed to get Oscar back up to the road and on a horse pointed down into the warm desert.

"I'm going to try and climb up to the horses and find a place to ride down here," he said. "I seem to remember that this gorge widens out pretty soon so that a man can reach it on horseback. Look up there."

He pointed at the slope and even in the darkness it was clear that it became more gradual. "I can climb that and maybe beat the sheriff to our horses."

Oscar nodded. "Good," he whispered. "Go ahead. I'll be all right."

Clint wanted to make sure that his instructions were clearly understood. "I want you to catch your breath and then follow my path. Climb as high as you can, then turn downriver and start moving along the slope. I'll find you a mile or two below. It will save us a lot of time. Also, if you're up on the side, I'll be able to find you easier."

"What about the sheriff? Maybe he'll be able to find me first."

Clint paused. Oscar's fears were legitimate. Sheriff Gray would probably need to hike down near this point in order to climb out and reach the horses. Hopefully, Clint would reach the road first and maybe he'd even come face to face with the corrupt lawman. But Clint could not be sure and there was no sense in trying to con Oscar into thinking his life wasn't in real danger.

"If he crosses your path, I might not be able to help you, Oscar. You'll have to fight him. Either that, or I'll have to stay with you and hope that . . ."

Oscar looked squarely into Clint's eyes. In the gloom and thunder of the river, he looked like a thoroughly beaten man. His clothes were ripped, his face and ponderous body were bleeding from a dozen scratches and abrasions. He looked old and fat and extremely vulnerable. But how he looked was not the measure of the man.

"No," he said with his teeth gritted in pain. "I've had enough of this! If he tries to kill me . . . I will try to kill him back—as God is my witness!"

Clint reached out and patted the man on his bare shoulder. Oscar's flesh felt ice cold. "If he comes, try to gain the higher ground. Then do what he did, grab a big rock and throw it at his head."

"I've never thrown anything at anyone."

"I know. But it's easy if you try. Remember what he did to us. He won't give you any quarter—his job, probably even his life depend on stopping us from getting out of here alive."

Clint stood up and his eyes tracked the best line out of the canyon. "It'll be light within an hour. With luck, I'll find Gray before he finds you. And then I'll meet you downriver. We'll be sweltering in the desert heat by noon tomorrow."

Oscar nodded. He managed to raise one hand limply as a parting salute. Clint waved back and then attacked the canyonside. He had not told Oscar this, but there were rifles in the saddle scabbards of the two horses that they had taken from the main street of Piney. If the sheriff got ahold of those rifles first, he and Oscar were dead men.

He moved up the canyonside as fast as he could but even though it was steeper, the rock was just as loose. For every three steps Clint took foreward, he slipped back two. Every muscle of his body felt tortured. One hip pained him badly and the shoulder which Gray had hit with a big rock was throbbing and becoming stiff.

Clint tried not to think about his pain. He goaded himself into maximum effort by remembering that his life and that of Oscar depended upon him reaching the horses first.

But now and again he had to stop to catch his breath. Each time he did, he would pear back down the slope and try to see Oscar or the sheriff. He saw neither.

The last hundred feet were an agony. The strength in his legs was gone so he crawled and pulled himself up to the road with the dwindling strength of his arms. When he topped the rise, he halfway expected the sheriff to be standing there with a rifle pointed at his head. The man would say something like, "Nice try, Gunsmith, but you lose." Then, he would pull the trigger and the force of the slug would send Clint's body tumbling in a landslide of loose rock all the way to the bottom of the gorge.

Clint pushed to his feet. He raised his head and took one step, then another. The road was steep and he had a good mile to walk back to the horses, but after his climb up from the river, it seemed very easy. His confidence and strength grew with each long swinging stride.

Chapter Twenty-Nine

Oscar Marsh had waited until the Gunsmith disappeared into the predawn darkness before deciding to move. He didn't want to, and every step he took was agony. This was, he thought, a miserable situation for a gentleman in retirement to endure. He had never imagined he would ever be involved in all the terrible things that had occurred during the past forty-eight hours. First that terrifying wagon ride down the mountainside and then those rifle shots that had sent him and the poor driver careening over the cliff. It was really quite unimaginable. And now, having somehow escaped drowning in this awful river, he still faced the threat of being killed by a half-insane sheriff.

Oscar listened carefully to discover if the man was anywhere close, but it was impossible to hear anything over the river.

Had Clint been successful in scaling this mountainside? Would they truly escape this bone-numbing cold and wetness to bask in the heat of the desert by this afternoon? It did not seem possible.

I must go on, Oscar told himself, rousing an unwilling body. He climbed a few feet more and rested when he began to shake with fatigue. He kept up that routine until daylight filtered weakly into the gorge and he began to see more clearly. Clint had been correct—the gorge did widen toward the desert floor. Oscar craned his head up and studied the wall of loose rock. He might even be able to scale it if he weren't so weary. He was encouraged to see that he had already climbed a long way up from the river below.

Oscar thought about how good it would be to get out of this cold, wet gorge. If only he could climb up to the road. It would make Clint's job of finding him that much easier. All that would be required would be to walk along the mountainside until he saw the Gunsmith coming with horses. Oscar knew that he had been a terrible bother so far. Clint had nearly drowned saving his life. It would be something to be proud of if he could surprise him by making it out under my own steam and saving him a ride down into this forbidding chasm.

That decided, Oscar began to work his way up toward the rim. He moved only a few yards at a time, stopping frequently to catch his breath. He had chosen a diagonally upward path that he thought he might be able to traverse. He sincerely believed he could make it out all by himself—until he heard a rock break loose not far below and twisted around to see Sheriff Gray.

Cold panic seized Oscar's heart in its icy grip. He began to claw at the loose shale and completely forgot his selected path. The loose rock shifted ominously under his body and instead of moving up, he found himself slowly edging downward toward the sheriff. They were less than sixty feet apart. With him slipping and the sheriff climbing, they would collide in minutes. Oscar fought the slope like a man gone wild.

The man had a killing look in his eyes and he growled, "Where is he? Where is the Gunsmith?"

"He's gone! He made it out to the horses." Oscar tore at the slope, dug his fingertips, his knees and his toes into the shifting rock in a desperate attempt to halt his slow descent. "Please, leave me alone!"

The sheriff was also having trouble with the rock, but

not as much. He picked up a rock the size of a canta-loupe and tried to hurl it at Oscar, but without solid footing, the rock fell short.

Even so, the act galvanized Oscar and he grabbed a rock of his own and twisted around so that his back was to the rockslide. "Get away or so help me I'll throw this at you!"

The sheriff did not even bother to respond. He found a firm place and managed to stand. Balancing precari-ously, he grabbed a smaller rock and hurled it with all of his strength. The rock struck Oscar's leg.

Oscar groaned, felt stinging tears in his eyes. "Damn you, why can't we act like civilized men!" he cried. Then, he hurled his own rock and missed by at least three feet.

When the sheriff laughed, Oscar grabbed another rock and tried not to humiliate himself by weeping like a helpless boy. "Stay back, I said. Please!"

The sheriff attacked the slope. He seemed to find the will and the strength to overcome it and moved steadily upward. Oscar shook with terror. He outweighed the man considerably but knew very well that he was far older and weaker. And he knew without a doubt that the sheriff had killed before and would not hesitate to kill now.

Oscar hurled his second rock with all the fading strength in his flabby arm. The sheriff, breath tearing in and out of his lungs, heard the loose rock begin to rattle as the slope shifted again. He straightened up and the rock struck him squarely in the nose. He cried out in pain and then lost his balance and toppled backward.

The developing landslide from above caught up with his body and the entire slope began to cut loose from its foundation. Oscar hung just above the slide and watched as an immense cloud of rock dust billowed up to obscure everything. Large boulders farther down broke free and crashed together. The force of the slide grew steadily and rumbled until the entire gorge trembled.

And then suddenly, it all stopped. The slide had hit the bottom of the gorge and momentarily damned the river. Oscar stared down at the dust and when it finally begin to settle, he saw a huge new dam. The river filled behind and then scaled the dam and continued its race toward the desert floor.

Oscar's wet, bloodshot eyes searched for the body of Sheriff Gray, knowing that the man was buried beneath tons of loose shale and rock. He buried his round face in his bloody hands and cried. But soon, he twisted around and relocated his original path to the road above. He told himself again and again that he was not a murderer—in a court of law, he would be found innocent and the verdict would be that he acted in self defense. But how did he judge himself?

Clint heard the landslide and turned in time to see the immense cloud of dust rising from the gorge. He considered going immediately back to investigate, but decided that he had better get to the horses first before the sheriff or someone else found them. All he could do was say a quick prayer that Oscar had not been buried.

The horses were right where he had left them hidden. Clint grabbed a rifle and checked that it was loaded and in good working order. Satisfied, he mounted and started down the road, leading the extra horse.

When he arrived above the rock slide, he forced his reluctant horse to move up close to the edge of the road. No one could have been more surprised than he was to see Oscar Marsh less than fifty feet below.

Clint uncoiled the rope on his saddle and yelled, "Grab hold and I'll pull you on up!"

Oscar was too winded to answer but his face showed his relief. He caught the rope on Clint's second throw and tied it around his ample waist. Clint turned his horse and it had to work hard to pull him up and over the lip. Oscar flopped spread-eagled out on the road. Clint dismounted and rolled the man over on his back.

"Are you all right?"

Oscar nodded. "I am now."

"Have you seen the sheriff?"

Oscar nodded again and, in as few words as possible, told him what had happened to Gray. When he was finished with the story, Clint said, "Well, he deserved what he got but I sure wish we could have used him against Abraham Bolt. I'll bet he knew all sorts of things that man has done."

Oscar rolled over and then sat up. "I have never been so filthy and miserable," he said. "Could we go now? I want to find someplace to take a bath and soak. And I need new clothes and . . ."

"Whoa!" Clint said. "Before we do anything, we have to think about what's happening back up on the Mogollon Rim. Abraham isn't going to sit still and wait for us to bring a judge and United States Marshal up to shackle his hands and send him off to prison."

Oscar scowled. "You're right," he said quietly. "Well, what should we do?"

Clint expelled a deep breath. "You won't like what I have to say."

"I'll help Dinah Morgan in any way I can. Tell me exactly what is required."

"All right. I think the time has passed for legal action saving anyone. I sure can't go back to jail, not with the sheriff killed. And those charges of assault against Abraham you intended to file, hell, that man will never go to trial either."

"What are you trying to tell me, Clint?"

"Just this. The time for lawyers and judges is past. It's war up here now and I have to go back and try to stop Abraham from wiping Dinah's Place off the map. There isn't time to visit Phoenix."

"There is always time for the law. We have to take

the time," Oscar argued wearily.

"Like you did down on that slope against the sheriff?" Clint shook his head, immediately regretting his words. "I'm sorry. That wasn't fair to you. But you see my point. Sometimes you just don't have the luxury of taking the time to do things the right—the legal—way. Not out in the west, you don't."

Oscar swallowed noisily. He stared down into the gorge and Clint noticed how much the man had changed in the last two days. He appeared to have lost forty pounds. He was all banged up and his clothes were hanging off him in threads. But he looked resolute and hard, somehow. He looked like a realist instead of a damned idealist.

"All right," Oscar said quietly. "You win. Let's go back to Dinah's Place while we still can."

A wide grin split Clint's features and he slapped the man on the back. "Now you're talking, pardner! Let's ride."

Chapter Thirty

Dinah's Place was just as calm and picturesque as he had seen it last. Clint breathed a sigh of relief to see Dinah and her guests busy at work on the cabins.

"Our luck is still holding," he told Oscar as they rode out of the trees and onto the huge, meadow with its tall grass. "Abraham and his men must still be searching for me nearer to town."

"Do you really think he would dare to attack these people?"

"I'm sure he will," Clint said. "It's not a matter of 'if' but of 'when.' "

Dinah Morgan saw them as they emerged into the open. She waved excitedly but then froze as a powerful rifle boomed from ambush. Clint felt the impact of a lead ball rip him out of the saddle. His entire left side went numb. His skull burned. He felt as if some giant bird had used its talons to pluck him up by the head then hurled him to the earth.

"Clint!" Oscar Marsh piled off his horse, stumbled, fell then regained his feet and came racing toward him as gunfire bracketed the resort.

Clint tried to climb to his feet but his legs were like butter.

"Stay down!" Oscar shouted, throwing himself at Clint as the powerful hunting rifle boomed again. They

158

were falling just as a second heavy slug whip-cracked past Clint's ear. For a moment, Clint lay still in the grass feeling the numbness began to wear off and be replaced by a tingling sensation. He looked at Oscar and whispered, "Poke your head up and tell me what you see, then get as far away from me as you can."

"And let them find and kill you?" Oscar sneered. "Not a chance. You saved my life, now it's time I helped save yours. Can you move?"

Clint nodded, hearing the gunfire escalate in its intensity. "I think so. But what's going on!"

Oscar poked his head up. "Dinah's Place is under attack from two sides. The guests are racing for cover and . . . and I see riders with torches! They're firing our new cabins!"

"Get me a horse," Clint whispered. "I have to get on a horse and help them!"

Oscar nodded. "Ours didn't run very far, I'll try to catch them." Oscar began to crawl through the tall grass with surprising speed for a man his age and size. In less than a minute, he came rushing back on foot leading one of their stolen horses.

"Get out of here before they come for you!" the law professor pleaded, grabbing Clint and helping him into the saddle.

Clint could feel blood running down from his scalp. The bullet must have grazed his skull and he was so dizzy it was all he could do to hang on to the saddlehorn.

"Run!" Oscar yelled, "they're coming this way now!"

Clint lifted his head. He had to close one eye to focus. The Bolt raiders were firing the cabins but were apparently under orders not to kill anyone. Even so, they were frightening to behold and were having great sport in hazing the guests, wrecking the dock and shooting holes to sink all of the resort's rowboats.

160

"Damn them!" Clint hissed as he tried to pull the rifle out of it's scabbard and failed. "Dammit anyway!"

"Run!" Oscar screamed as he threw himself headlong back into the tall grass.

The very last thing in the world that Clint wanted to do was to run but he had seen enough men grazed by a bullet to know the temporary effects would not last more than a few hours. Then, he could fight. But now, as he watched Abraham Bolt wheel his horse and come charging across the meadow to finish him off, Clint knew that he had very little choice but to escape with his life.

He spurred his horse back toward the nearby wall of forest. Bullets swarmed after him. The horse he rode was already exhausted from hard riding and even though it was game, the animal was painfully slow. Clint hung on and let the horse carry him deeper and deeper into the heavy timber. He glanced back and saw that Abraham had ordered his riders to fan out; they were like flitting shadows in the murky shade of pines. He knew that they were moving up swiftly to overtake him.

Clint made a snap decision and, choosing a soft-looking place beside a rotting log, he jumped. The impact was jarring and he almost lost consciousness as he rolled up against the log. With his rifle still in his fists, he struggled to dig himself under the log. Several moments later, horses on the run swept by leaving the forest silent in their wake.

They would be coming back soon. Clint knew perfectly well that they would chase down the riderless horse and begin to backtrack. I have to move laterally to their path, he thought, rolling out from under the tree and climbing to his feet.

He swayed and the world tilted crazily but it did not flip or roll. Clint took one step, then another. He could walk. With his eyes fixed ahead, he began to move as quickly as he could, intending to make a loop through the forest that would return him to Mirror Lake.

"If they've killed anyone," Clint whispered, "Abraham Bolt is as good as dead right now."

The lake was calm, and clouds hung white and serene against a backdrop of azure sky.

Even the bluejays in the trees were calling raucously back and forth among themselves to indicate that the danger had passed. Clint stepped out of forest with his rifle up and ready. He was in bad shape. The river and gorge had taken a heavy toll on his strength and the new scalp wound had left him feeling as if his very bones were made of crushed egg shells. He stared across the lake at the pillars of smoke that lifted from what had been cabins. Nothing stood, not even the rock fireplaces and tin stove chimneys. All of it had been roped and dragged to the ground. He could see the guests huddled together on the grass like frightened sheep.

She has lost, Clint thought, remembering how Dinah had mortgaged everything including the land to buy the timber and materials for those new cabins. Even after I kill Abraham Bolt, she has still lost everything.

Clint gritted his teeth with each step for the pain in his head was unremitting. He wondered if anyone had been killed in the attack or if Abraham had been content to just scare them all enough to finally drive them away.

When he finally reached them, he saw that they were all gathered together in the meadow around a freshly dug grave. Clint felt his stomach muscles cramp violently. He was too late and Abraham had killed Dinah Morgan. He was wrong.

Dinah came to her feet and when she saw him, her composure gave away and she rushed to enfold him in her arms.

Clint held her for a long moment and then he pushed

her gently away and stared at the grave. "Is it Oscar?" he managed to say.

"Yes," Dinah choked, "they made him tell them what happened to the sheriff and then they were going to hang him from a tree. He fought them so hard they ended up shooting him instead."

Clint swallowed feeling a knot in his throat. "Who did it, Abraham?"

"A new gunfighter on the Bolt payroll named Quince. He's the one that suggested they take Ben and keep him until I deeded over my land and left the Mogollon Rim forever."

"They took Ben!"

Dinah nodded dully. "Abraham swore that nothing would happen to my son if we all left tomorrow. He made me sign over every bit of this to him for the consideration of one dollar."

"Where can we get him?"

"He'll be in Piney tomorrow. And there was one other thing, Clint. Abraham said that you have to be the man to come and take him."

Clint felt himself stiffen inside. He stared at Dinah who was beaten, face blackened and obviously in a state of shock. The guests weren't much better off. Some of the women were whimpering and Mr. Hammer had a nasty bruise along one side of his face that said he had at least tried to resist the attackers.

Clint moved over to Oscar Marsh's grave and knelt beside it. He took a handful of the rich, loamy soil and squeezed it until his fingers bled as he remembered a man he had come to respect and admire during the last few days they had spent together.

"I give you my word, Oscar," he breathed, "they will pay for this!"

Chapter Thirty-One

Clint stood and faced the guests. Someone had to explain things and try to make them understand what was going on.

"We have all worked together," he began, "each doing what they could to help build this resort for Dinah, and for ourselves. I know that you people didn't come here to be chased and shot at by men on horseback. And you are probably feeling every bit as sick about the death of Oscar Marsh as I am. But I want you to know something very important."

Clint paused for a moment, his eyes studying each man and woman. "Oscar saved my life yesterday out here in this meadow, and he did it because he wanted me to beat Abraham Bolt and give this country law and justice. Until Dinah came, the man ruled the Mogollon Rim with an iron fist.

"No one dared cross him. He was so confident that he never even bothered to acquire a title to this beautiful lake—he just made the decision that it was his, and that was that. The man is a killer, and now a kidnapper. I intend to get Ben back and kill Abraham so we can all be done with this."

Clint glanced over at the grave. "For Oscar's sake, I ask you not to run away. Stand beside Dinah and help her rebuild. We can raise more money, but we need help."

Frank Hammer stepped forward. "I tried to help and all I got was a stirrup in the face. I'm not a young man anymore. Not half the man I was twenty years ago. I'd like to live out my normal lifespan, Gunsmith."

Clint nodded with understanding. "We all would, but there's a boy's life at stake."

"Abraham wouldn't dare kill him," someone said. "In fact, if we just leave, then the boy will be safer. If we don't do as Mr. Bolt asks, we could risk Ben's life."

"No!" Dinah cried with her fists clenched. "That is exactly what Abraham would have us believe. He wants us to play it safe. He wants Clint to come for my son and then he will kill the Gunsmith. After that, he can do what he wants with us knowing there is no one to stop him. The law is dead on the Mogollon Rim now."

"This land, this lake," a woman argued hotly, "it isn't worth risking one hair on Ben's head!"

"Ben's grandmother and grandfather fought and died for this land!" Dinah said, her voice shaking. "Yes, it is worth fighting and dying for.

"Ben knows that. Someday, it will be his, and then his children's. He loves this place. You've all seen how he knows every good fishing place, every secret meadow and stream for miles around. This is our home. With or without these cabins, this is our home!"

Dinah took a deep breath. "And we are going to fight for it with or without your help."

"And what if your son is killed because of that?" a woman demanded. "Can you live with yourself?"

Dinah stared past the woman toward the lake. For a long time, she was quiet and then she said, "I don't honestly know the answer to that one, Mrs. Quarry. I won't let it come to that."

Clint stepped up beside her. "Bolt wants us to come into Piney tomorrow and get Ben. Tomorrow is too late. I'm going to rescue the boy tonight."

"We are going to rescue my son tonight," Dinah corrected.

Frank Hammer stepped forward even though his wife tried to pull him back. "I'll go with you."

He turned to his wife. "I've got to," he said gently as he patted her hand. "If I don't go, I'll never be able to face myself in the mirror. I won't be worth a damn to myself or anyone else. Please understand."

His wife nodded and her chin lifted. "You always have made me proud of you, Frank. And right now, I'm proudest of all."

Clint said, "I can use help. But only as a last resort. I'd need men to stay well out from the Bolt Ranch headquarters and either cover our leaving with Ben, or else to set up a diversion of some kind. I won't have you anyone of you go face to face with Bolt's crew of hardcases. But then too, I can't guarantee that no one will be hurt out there."

"We appreciate your honesty, Clint," a man named Bill said, "but each of us knows there is no such thing as guarantees in life. Count me in with you."

"Me too," another man said loudly.

More men stepped forward and Clint was proud of them, even the ones who were not physically fit to go off on such a quest.

To those men, he said, "Your bravery is a tribute to your name. But I think we have enough already."

A couple of them protested so vigorously that Clint relented and allowed them to come along. Three others, however, understood that their age and condition would prove to be more of a liability than a help and they were easily persuaded to remain and defend the women guests.

Clint sized up his small army of oldsters. He felt pretty old himself with his injured hip, shoulder and his skull still pounding fiercely. "Can all of you hit what you aim at with a sixgun or a rifle?" he asked.

Six of them nodded, the others indicated they could, but that they were poor shots.

"Let's have a quick shooting lesson," Clint said.

"Collect every weapon on the place and bring them here."

The guests had all managed to gather their belongings before the cabins had been fired. They had guns, but no one had been foolish enough to attempt to use them against Bolt's professionals. Now, as Clint inspected the weapons, he wondered if he was doing the right thing by involving all of these old men.

Clint sat a row of tin cans up in front of the smoky ashes of a burned out cabin. He ordered each man to step forward and fire. Hammer and several others were pretty fair shots, but most of the others were just pot-shoters. Men who knew enough about a gun to defend themselves or their property, but no more.

"Are you having second thoughts about them?" Dinah asked quietly.

Clint watched the men practice. "No," he said. "All I hope we'll need from them is smoke and noise. Something to distract and maybe give us a covering fire if we get into trouble."

Dinah nodded. "I just want you to know one thing, Clint. We are doing this together, all the way. I'm not going to let you go into the ranch house alone."

"All right." Clint knew there was no sense in trying to talk Dinah into remaining on the perimeter of fire with her guests. "I've seen enough of this. Why don't you tell us all you know about the Bolt Ranch head-quarters? How it is situated so that we have a good idea of what we can expect to find."

Clint yelled, "Hold your fire! Gather around and let's map some strategy."

Dinah knelt beside the lake with a pointed stick in her hand. On the wet dirt of the shoreline, she drew a detailed map of the Bolt Ranch. "This is called Crossfire Mountain after a famous battle there many years ago in which Abraham Bolt was supposed to be trapped between two bands of Indians. Over here is another mountain and down in between is the ranch house and all the buildings.''

"Draw them exactly as you remember," Clint said quietly as the stick created the picture.

Dinah drew without any hesitation. She seemed to know exactly how the ranch buildings were arranged. This would have surprised Clint and raised some questions if he had not known about her youthful relationship with Johnny Bolt. Obviously, Johnny had either drawn a similar map many times, or else they had sneaked in close enough to the ranch to see it. One thing for sure, Abraham would not have allowed even the daughter of a Morgan to set foot on his ranch.

When she was finished, Clint studied the map carefully. "Where are the ranch horses kept?''

"I'm sorry, I forgot to draw in the corrals. Here," Dinah said, jabbing the stick into the soft mud.

"Good."

Clint took the stick and touched Crossfire Mountain. "Here is the weakness. This mountain comes right down to the back of the ranch house and it gives us the cover we need and also the advantage of elevation. Also, we'll want a few men here, here and here," he said, marking small circles a considerable distance out from the ranch buildings.

Clint looked at each of his volunteers. "Dinah and I will sneak in just before dawn. We'll find Ben and bring him out as the sun pops over the eastern horizon. If everything goes the way I hope, not a shot will be fired. We'll bring Ben to Piney and all meet in the church at the end of town. Abraham won't dare attack us or try to burn down his own church."

"But he and that sonofabitch, Quince, they won't let us just walk away winners," Hammer snarled.

"No," Clint agreed, "he won't. But you'll all have done your jobs. When Abraham and Quince come, it will be time for me to finish up business."

They understood his meaning.

"What about Abraham's son, Johnny?" one of the guests asked. "You going to kill him too?"

Clint glanced sideways at Dinah who looked away quickly. "Not unless I have to," he answered quietly.

Dinah whispered, "If he tries to kill you or keep my son a hostage for any reason whatsoever, I will shoot him myself."

They all looked toward Dinah. Her hair hung in her face and she looked haggard but very, very determined. So grimly determined that not one among them didn't believe she would do exactly as she promised.

Clint nodded and felt better for knowing exactly how the cards might fall. A woman like Dinah was complicated. He knew she still loved the father of her son, but he wanted to make sure that she also knew he was not going to risk his own life if Johnny Bolt decided to fight side by side with his father.

Johnny was caught on the fence. Before this was all over, he was just going to have to come down on one side or the other. It was hard to imagine him going against his father, but he might if he knew that Ben was his son.

Clint didn't like jokers in his card game—especially when the stakes were counted in lives.

He stretched and then began to pull off his boots, shirt and socks. He was filthy and had sore muscles. The lake was going to feel good and so was the nap he intended to take afterward.

"Wake me up when it gets dark," he told them. "Try to get some sleep yourselves. We've got a long night ahead of us."

Dinah and the guests nodded and their eyes widened a little to see all the cuts and bruises that purpled his body. Clint did not care. The water of Mirror Lake would sooth his muscles and clear his throbbing head. By midnight when they rode out for Ben, he would be fine. And one way or the other, this thing would be over and he could begin to enjoy life once more.

Idly, he wondered about how Harold Westerfield was getting along in Flagstaff. It was a good thing that Harold had decided to move on to another resort to enjoy and then write his magazine article. Maybe, Clint thought, I can figure out some way to salvage Dinah's Place when this is all said and done.

He saw a big fish flop against the clear blue water. So what if Dinah's cabins were destroyed. They could be rebuilt bigger and better than ever by next spring. Cabins were replaceable, but not something like these meadows and this lake. No sirree!

Clint just had a feeling that if he could kill Abraham Bolt and rescue Ben, Dinah's Place would be back in business for next year's tourist season and for years to come.

Chapter Thirty-Two

There weren't enough horses for everyone so Clint had some of the lighter men double up. It was just past midnight and there was so much nervousness among them that Clint was sure one of the old men would accidently shoot himself to death before the night was over.

"All right," he said, standing before them in the moonlight, "there isn't much left to say. We stay close together right up until we're within a mile of Bolt headquarters, then we split up. You all know where you are supposed to be and which horses to keep close by. I don't want any shots fired unless we are seen and must defend ourselves. And make sure that everyone has a horse to get away on. Nobody gets left in the dark. Is that understood?"

They nodded solemnly. Clint had spent the last hour going over and over what they had to do and he was finally convinced that these men understood their roles perfectly. Their wives had been his biggest problem, some of them had changed their minds and begged their husbands to remain behind. Two men had succumbed to their pleas, but the rest had held firm.

"I want to say one more thing. If shooting starts, we've got them in a crossfire. And if we hold them, they can't escape. According to Dinah, there is plenty of open ground between the buildings and the forest. They won't be eager to cross it after daybreak.''

"What if we hear gunfire inside the ranch house?''

"Good question,'' Clint said. "If you do, that means that Dinah and I have been discovered trying to rescue the boy. We can still get out but the light will be poor, so don't fire until you are sure that it's not us that you're aiming at!''

"If it is you're not likely to get hit,'' someone muttered cryptically. "Not a one of us can shoot worth a damn anymore.''

The resulting ripple of laughter helped to ease the tension. "Everyone gets lucky sometime,'' Clint said. "You might even hit what you aim for tomorrow morning and surprise yourselves. The important thing is that you are there to cover us in case we need help. After we are gone, then each of you get back on a horse and ride for the church in Piney where your wives are waiting.''

"Before we leave,'' Dinah added, "I want to thank you with all my heart. I know you're not doing this for shares or stock in my resort or for any reason other than that you are brave, decent men. And no matter how tonight comes out, I love you each and every one.''

Clint figured those were as good parting words as any. They made his throat tighten a little and he imagined some of the old men were kind of choked up too. Anyway, he swung aboard Duke feeling good to be back on top of his own horse once more. Dinah maneuvered in beside him and they headed toward the Bolt Ranch riding stirrup to stirrup.

Twice, Clint twisted around in his saddle and glanced at the old men on their gentle old plug horses, some of them riding singly, others two to a horse. "I must be crazy leading this bunch off to fight,'' he said, half aloud and half just to himself.

Dinah heard him. She also glanced back over her shoulder at the men who followed. "I know these people, Clint. Right now, they're more alive than they have been in years. This may be the most exciting thing they've done in their entire lives.''

''And the dumbest.''

She reached out and touched his cheek with her fingertips. ''You don't believe that for a minute. It's Ben we are after, nothing else counts. Certainly not my land or my life.''

''We'll get Ben,'' he vowed. ''And before this is over, I'll make sure that you never have to worry about Abraham Bolt again.''

''Do you know the gunfighter by the name of Quince?''

''No,'' he said. ''But they come and they go real fast, Dinah. This one has a debt to pay for killing Oscar.''

''But it is Ben that's most important,'' she reiterated.

He nodded understanding her concern that he might lose sight of the purpose of all this. ''Yes, first we get your son out of there, and back in Piney—then I take care of Quince and Abraham Bolt.''

They rode on in silence for awhile before she said, ''You seem so very sure that you can kill them. Tell me, does a gunfighter of your stature always feel so confident?''

''Has to or he'll be killed right away.''

Clint glanced up at the full moon. There were clouds in the sky tonight and some of them might scud across the moon and suddenly plunge the night into absolute darkness. He would have to keep an eye on them for they could work both for or against their purposes.

''Have you ever thought about . . . getting married? Settling down and raising a family? Building something permanent and important?''

''Like a tourist resort?''

''Yes. How did you guess?''

He chuckled softly. ''I'd like that fine in about another five or ten years. But not now. To be real honest with you, Dinah, I've seen enough of the tourist business to last me at least until next summer."

"Not likely I'll be in business then."

"Sure you will. After we get rid of Abraham and his threat is gone, you'll have people falling all over themselves trying to invest in Dinah's Place."

"I'll give these men behind us the first chance to bankroll me if they want," she said. "In return, I'll give them a share of the resort and free land with a view of the lake."

"Free land!" Clint softly whistled in feined amazement. "My, you're getting very generous."

"Yes, I suppose. But I'll reserve the right to charge them a small use fee. That only seems fair, doesn't it?"

"Sounds fair to me," he said stifling a laugh and thinking that he had never met a woman who had such a mind for snatching up dollars.

"Good! Then that's how we'll do it," she said with a decisive shake of her head. "My only regret is that I will never get written up in the *New York Gentleman's Quarterly* and have all those rich easterners flocking out to enjoy the beauty of the Mogollon Rim. Bringing their beautiful money to spend so that Piney can finally turn into something besides Bolt's own little watering hole."

Clint thought about that. "You know," he said, "I might just go to Flagstaff and find Harold. I don't have to tell him about what happened. None of this."

"He'd kill you if he wrote about my place not knowing there was nothing left of it but ashes and the dock."

"No he wouldn't," Clint said. "Besides, by the time he finally comes around again, it will be bigger and better than ever."

"You almost make me believe that."

Clint absently patted the sixgun on his hip. "Believe it," he said. "I aim to make it all come true."

Chapter Thirty-Three

Clint and Dinah waited until each group of men surrounding the ranch buildings struck a match to signal they were ready and in position. The last to signal were the ones on Crossfire Mountain because they had the farthest to go and were the most critical to his plan; being the closest, they were also the ones that he and Dinah would run to when they had Ben.

Clint looked up at the sky and wished clouds would have blocked out some of the bright moonlight that flooded the ranch. There was no way that they could get either to or from the ranch house without being highly visible. He debated waiting an hour or so and hoping that the clouds would do his bidding, but then he decided to go now and take their chances.

"Have you ever been inside?" he asked.

"No," Dinah answered, "but I think the bedrooms are on the west side. At least . . . at least Johnny's is. He pointed it out to me one night."

"I expect he's inside, Dinah. I hope it's clear in your mind what to do if he tries to stop us."

Her face hardened. "I won't hesitate to do what's necessary to save my son's life."

"Good." The ranch was laid out exactly as Dinah had sketched it in the mud of Mirror Lake. Clint studied the bunkhouse, the cook shack and the corrals. For the final time, his mind went over what would happen if a shot were fired to alert the hands that there was danger. Clint returned his attention to the Bolt ranch house once more. It was big. The original log cabin had been added on to so many times over the years that it was now just the kitchen. "I hope we can find Ben without having to open every door."

"Can we go now?" Dinah asked. She wore a gun on her shapely hip which Clint knew that she would not hesitate to use.

"Okay, let's do it."

Clint stayed in the trees as he headed for a shallow draw. The draw brought them as close to the ranch as they were going to get before they had to step out onto open ground. He and Dinah moved quickly down the hillside and past the barn into the ranch yard. Clint's nerves were on a hair-trigger edge as he and Dinah hurried across the yard toward the front door. They skirted several wagons in various states of disrepair and had to pass through what had once been a gate but now was just a broken frame of pickets.

In the moonlight, Clint could see that this ranch had once known the care of a woman's touch. There were roses gone wild and the faint outline of a garden long since gone to seed.

A few flower pots lay broken and scattered around the yard.

They reached the door without incident. Clint tried the knob and found it unlocked. He took a deep breath and stepped inside the house, then reached back and grabbed Dinah's hand and moved out of the open doorway.

It was much darker inside. Clint waited for his eyes to adjust a little better and when several minutes had passed and he still could not see much of anything, he reached into his vest pocket and drew out a wooden match.

"Take out your gun and be ready for anything," he whispered, as he cupped the match and fired it with his thumbnail.

The light jumped out and brightly illuminated the room for an instant, then it sputtered and Clint's hands choked off most of its glow. Dinah saw a candle close by and brought it back to Clint to use. They stood for a minute looking about the room, trying to get their bearings before they began to search for Ben.

The living room in which they stood was cluttered with harness and saddles that were being repaired in the evenings when it was too dark to work outside. A massive rock fireplace took up an entire wall and over it hung the head and antlers of a magnificent elk. There were a lot of guns and even a few Indian bows and spears nailed to the wall. Cowhide rugs covered a filthy pine floor and the furniture was broken and worn.

They had already agreed to stay together and search the bedrooms but now Dinah hissed, "Why don't we split up so we can do this quickly and get out of here!"

"No," he said with a shake of his head. "We stick together."

"But there are hallways of rooms going off in both directions!"

"We'll have to trust to luck we find the right ones first thing. Come on." This was no time for them to be debating anything. Clint led off with the candle in one hand and his gun in the other.

They barely opened the first bedroom door and peeked inside. Just enough light from the candle slanted in to reveal a man asleep face down on the bed.

They passed on quickly to find the next room empty. Clint pushed open the third door and peered inside to see a man sleeping beside a long-haired Mexican woman. They stirred and he pulled his candle away quickly then closed the door feeling sweat bead on his forehead. This was ten times worse than just facing up to a man and settling things sudden-like. Clint knew that most of his anxiety was caused by the knowledge that, if he failed, not only was his life forfeit, but so too were the lives of Dinah and Ben.

They came to the last bedroom in this hallway and Clint's palm felt damp when he inched the heavy door open a crack and peeked inside. There was enough moonlight streaming through the room to see Johnny Bolt asleep on the bed and close by on a horsechair sofa a much smaller figure. Ben.

Clint reached back and squeezed Dinah's arm hard enough to let her know that they had found her son. He blew out their candle, then eased the door open and moved inside the room on tiptoes with Dinah right behind him. Clint reached the sofa and bent down beside the boy. For a moment, he hesitated, afraid that Ben might cry out in fright. He had no choice but to clamp a silencing hand over the boy's mouth.

Ben did scream, but most of the sound of it was muffled. For an instant, Ben's face reflected terror and he stared unseeing. But then, he recognized Clint and his body went limp as Clint lifted him up. He would carry Ben outside before putting him down to run. A half-asleep child was all too likely to knock something over in this house and ruin everything.

Clint heard Dinah take a sharp breath and then cock the hammer to her gun. He spun around helplessly with Ben in his arms.

Johnny was sitting up with a sixgun in his fist.

The gun was pointing right at Clint's face.

"Put him back down and he'll not be hurt," Johnny said, "do it right now, or I'll blow the top of your head off where you stand."

Clint glanced sideways at Dinah. The gun was still in her fist, but it was pointed at the floor.

An icy chill went through the Gunsmith's body. It appeared that he had made a very fatal error in judgement.

Chapter Thirty-Four

Dinah seemed to pull herself out of a trance. The gun lifted in her hand and she pointed it right at Johnny's broad chest. "No," she whispered hoarsely, "you put your gun down or I'll kill you, so help me God!"

"I don't believe you could."

Seconds dragged past like years. There was no sound in the room but their breathing until Dinah cocked the gun in her fist and said, "I'm taking my boy. Johnny, I don't want to kill you, but if you try and stop us, I will. Now, for the very last time, put down your gun and go back to sleep. Pretend this is a dream."

"What will I tell my father in the morning when he discovers that Ben is gone?"

"I don't care."

"You would if you were me. I can't betray my own father."

Clint had heard enough. "You have no choice. She'll kill you if you try to stop us."

Johnny did not even look in Clint's direction when he said, "I still don't think that you could do that, Dinah."

The gunbarrel in her fist began to shake violently as she extended it out to arm's length to pull the trigger.

Johnny quickly shoved his gun towards her and nodded. "All right. I'll go back to sleep. But first, I want you to know I had nothing to do about raiding your place and kidnapping Ben. Abraham sent me away to buy some cattle. By the time I got back, Ben was here and I made sure he stayed with me. I'd never have let them hurt him, Dinah.''

Tears made her eyes glisten and she nodded.

"Get his gun and let's go!" Clint said urgently as he pushed past them carrying the boy in his arms.

It was pitch black out in the hallway again without a candle. Clint cussed silently to himself as he groped forward wishing to hell that Dinah would relight that candle and come along. He felt pretty sure that Johnny wouldn't betray them, but until they were out in the yard then safely back among their friends on nearby Crossfire Mountain, he trusted nothing.

He reached the end of the hallway and turned right toward the door. But he had forgotten a pile of harness being repaired. The toe of Clint's boot got tangled up in the harness and with the boy in his arms, he tried to catch his balance but went crashing into a rifle rack. The glass front shattered as rifles spilled out and Clint went sprawling. He heard shouts and then running feet. "Ben!" he shouted into the darkness.

Dinah screamed in the hallway. Somewhere in the house, Abraham bellowed like a wild animal and Clint fought to untangle his feet from the cussed harness. Candle and lamp light flooded both hallways and Clint lunged for Ben and pushed him flat to the floor.

A gunshot filled the hall and Dinah screamed again. Suddenly, a slender man with sharp features burst into view. Clint swung his body around, his gun coming up. The man had Dinah and was using her as a shield! He fired at Clint and the Gunsmith dove behind a couch.

"Drop your gun!" Abraham shouted, from the opposite hallway.

Clint raised his head and the room rocked with the blast of a shotgun that blew the back of the couch to shreds. Clint flattened. He looked sideways at Ben who was just a few feet away and frozen with fear.

"Don't move," he whispered, hearing Abraham reloading his shotgun. Clint tried desperately to think of some way out of this trap. He had to act fast. Already, the men in the bunkhouse would be stumbling around searching for a light. In another couple of minutes they'd be coming with guns. And then, the game would be over.

Dinah must have known it as well because Clint could hear a terrible struggle going on in the hallway. He raised his head a fraction but Dinah and the man were too deep into the hall and he could not possibly help her. Again, the shotgun in Abraham's big hands boomed and Clint felt the couch take the impact. He snapped off a shot of his own but Abraham had ducked back into the hall and out of sight.

"Let her go, Quince!"

Clint swung around. It was Johnny's voice.

"No, goddammit, get. . . ."

A gun exploded and Dinah screamed. An instant later, the man named Quince staggered back into the living room, his gun down at his side. He tried to raise it to fire, but Johnny shot him twice more and he crashed over the shredded back of the couch.

The gunfighter's body sent Ben to his feet and before Clint could grab him, the confused boy ran straight into the hallway and Abraham's mighty arms crushed him. The old rancher bellowed. "It's over! Throw down your guns and come up or I blow this kid's brains all over the room!"

Clint bent his head in defeat. He had lost. There was not the slightest doubt in his mind that the hateful old man would do exactly as he said. Clint left his gun on the floor and stood up knowing he was going to die.

He looked right at Abraham Bolt. The man was dressed only in his underpants. His huge hairy body was bloated and wrinkled. His eyes burned with a fanatical kind of hatred. "So," he almost giggled, "I have you all!"

Clint tensed. Maybe if he tried to rush the man. . . .

"No, wait," Dinah called understanding what Clint was about to do. "Mr. Bolt, that boy is your grandson! Your grandson!"

Abraham rocked back on the heels of his bare feet. "You lying whore!"

"No, look at him! Do you see any resemblance to my late husband? Don't you see Johnny in his face and size? He's a Bolt!"

"He's a cursed Morgan!"

"No, he was conceived in Boston. That's why I was away a long time. To have Johnny's son."

Johnny took a step forward, the gun forgotten in his fist. He stared at Ben, first disbelieving and then with the growing realization that Dinah had to be telling the truth.

"Pa," he whispered, "he is my son! I . . . I know it's the truth!"

Abraham's face contorted with rage. "No!" he screamed. "No grandson of mine will come out of the belly of a Morgan, I'll kill him first!"

Ben struggled like a rabbit in a noose as Abraham tried to blow his head off. But aiming and firing a shotgun one-handed isn't easy. Abraham swore in frustration and dropped Ben to aim and fire as Clint scooped up his sixgun. There wasn't time to do anything more than fire off a wild and desperate snap shot.

Johnny Bolt also fired from the hip. No one was going to murder an innocent child—especially his son! Their guns echoed in one voice just as Abraham was swinging his shotgun toward little Ben Morgan.

Clint's bullet caught the poisonous old tyrant under the chin and traveled up through his brain to exit at the crown of his skull. Johnny's bullet drilled his father through the heart. Abraham reared backward, dead before his feet stopped shuffling. His body spasmed in death and the shotgun tilted upward and blew a hole in the roof before he crashed to lay twitching.

Ben ran to his mother and she clutched him to her and then they both went into Johnny's arms. The three of them hugged each other and that would have made a fine picture to end the night with except Clint heard running feet. He knew that within about fifteen seconds, there was going to be a hell of a lot more excitement when all the Bolt riders came rushing inside bent on emptying their sixguns.

Clint jumped for the front door and slammed it shut. It was heavy and he locked it a moment before someone hit it running. There were curses and then bullets began to rip splinters through the wood.

Clint stepped back where it was safer and said, "Sorry to break your reunion up, but, Johnny, you'd better have a word with those gunnies before someone else dies."

Johnny nodded. He pushed Dinah and the boy aside and called out, "It's all right in here. It's over. Go back to the bunkhouse."

"That you Johnny?" a man called. "Where's Abraham?"

"He's dead. It's over. Go back to the bunkhouse."

Clint could hear the brewing of long and heated argument. These men answered to Abraham, not to his son. But they did not know anything except that Johnny was alive and certainly Abraham dead or they'd have heard from him.

"All right, Boss," a man finally rumbled, "we'll talk in the morning."

"Yeah," Johnny said grimly as he stared at his dead father. "We'll do that."

Sunrise began to creep over the eastern horizon early that morning. Clint knuckled the grit from his eyes and stood in the ranchyard and made sure all of his old friends were in position. The bunkhouse was totally surrounded now. There was no escape.

The first of the Bolt men came out followed by the rest. There were fifteen of them and it was clear that they had not slept well. They looked disheveled and irritable. And they were armed.

"That's far enough," Clint said, as he and Johnny stepped out from behind a broken wagon. "Don't move for your guns, you're completely surrounded."

'Surrounded' was the key word agreed upon and the signal for all the oldsters to cock their weapons from their places of hiding.

The fifteen gunman froze except for their eyes which turned one way and then the other seeing the guns pointed at them.

"I'll make this real simple," Johnny said. "You're all fired. Every damn one of you. I'll have your guns now."

"You can't do this!"

Johnny sent a bullet whanging off the earth about a half inch from the man's boot. "Next one eats your big toe," he said matter-of-factly.

Clint grinned. It had been a fine shot and a nice line, one he'd remember. With a little practice, this fella might become quite a man after all! He watched the hired hands—men hired by Abraham on the basis of their gunskills rather than cowboying ability—make up their minds. They wisely chose to drop their guns and head for their horses.

When they rode out, Clint holstered his own gun and called in the old timers. Johnny Bolt had a lot of good brandy inside and it had been a long chilly night. Some of these old fellas were stiff as boards from their rheumatism. The brandy would warm them up and make everything all right again.

•   •   •

Clint sat atop of Duke and looked around at the Bolt ranch headquarters. He wondered if Johnny would stay here, or move on over and help Dinah and his son rebuild her resort. Knowing Dinah, Clint sort of guessed it would be the latter.

He said his goodbyes and rode off the Mogollon Rim heading for Flagstaff to find Harold Westerfield. He'd tell Harold that Dinah's Place was all finished up just fine. Best resort in Arizona.

Sure, that was stretching the truth plenty, but it wouldn't be by next spring. Johnny and Dinah would be married by then and she'd have her new husband with a hammer in his fist instead of a rope. Ben would have the father he needed and everything would be as it should.

On the last ridge, Clint reined Duke to a halt. Off through the trees, he could see Crossfire Mountain and about two miles out, catch a glimpse of Mirror Lake. He thought of Oscar Marsh and the kind of summer it was shaping up to be so far.

Exciting as always.

Made in the USA
Monee, IL
30 July 2021

74618031R00111